DRAGONFLY

Alice McLerran

"That is question now;
And then comes answer like an Absey book.
King John, i, 9
Shakespeare

Absey & Company
Spring, Texas

Library of Congress Cataloging-in-Publication Data

McLerran, Alice, 1933-
   Dragonfly / Alice McLerran.
      p. cm.
   Summary: After the mysterious egg they find hatches into a dragon, Jason, Philip, and Rose join their family and friends in a conspiracy to keep the growing creature a secret from the outside world.
   ISBN 1-888842-15-6 [1. Dragons--Fiction.] I. Title.

PZ7.M22534Dr2000
[Fic]--dc21   00-036274

Designed by Edward E. Wilson
Cover Art by Tristan Elwell

Dedication

For Stephen, David, and Rachel, in memory of all the adventures we shared.

Chapter 1

I don't know why I couldn't have been the one to find it instead of Rose. I was there, too. But she was poking around in the bushes—don't ask me why—and there it was: just that easy. "A dinosaur egg!" she squealed. Of course, she ran to get Philip. Philip's the big dinosaur expert; at least that's what he and Rose think.

Philip said it couldn't be a dinosaur egg because it wasn't a fossil. Well, I could have told her that. A fossil would be hard. This was tough and leathery, with a little give to it. Philip turned it over and around, doing the expert bit, taking his time. "I just don't know," he finally confessed. "The shape is like an egg, all right. Maybe an ostrich egg? I'm not sure what they're like. But that doesn't make sense. What would an ostrich be doing around here? ...I'm not sure WHAT it is." A big admission from The Voice of Authority.

"Well, whatever it is, it's mine. Right?" Rose was

looking at me. As though I were doing anything.

"Jason won't take it away from you," Philip assured her. I grinned, to keep her guessing.

"I'm going to put it in my bed," said Rose, "under the blankets. If it's some kind of egg, it might hatch if I keep it warm. And Jason, you stay out."

Big deal, threats from a baby. I quietly crossed my eyes at her, but she was busy with the egg and didn't notice.

The next morning, just as it was getting light outside, I woke up in the middle of a dream about an earthquake. No wonder: my whole bed was shaking. When I got my eyes open, I saw Rose dancing on the edge of my mattress, poking at the top bunk, trying to get Philip awake. "Wake up, Philip! Philip, come ON! Something's happening!"

It's almost impossible to wake Philip, so I got there first. Rose had pulled back the blankets on her bed, and the big egg was right in the middle of the sheet. It was trembling a little; something had to be moving around inside. Near the top there was a small tear in the leathery shell. When I got close, I could see a sharp little green claw sawing away from the inside. That slowed me down for a second—but I made myself step closer still, so I could get a better view.

By that time the other two were there, too. "It's hatching," said Philip, as though we couldn't see for ourselves.

2

We watched. Whatever was inside had almost fin-ished sawing a neat circle right around the top of the shell. "Hey, let's take off the lid!" I suggested.

"No," said Philip. "Leave it alone, let it do it itself."

"Don't touch it," said Rose, "It's MINE."

Just then the circle at the top of the egg lifted a little, and the thing inside started to crawl out. First a scaly little green foot with sharp claws; then a slender snout with flared nostrils; then the rest of the head, with big amber-colored eyes. Then another foot. Gradually, the rest of the front legs and a long neck. Then, with a sort of POP, two webbed wings. Whatever it was paused a minute to unfold and shake the wings. Then a sleek scaly body, and two more legs, and last of all a long scaly tail that ended in a sort of spade-shaped paddle emerged.

"It's a DRAGON!" cried Rose, "A baby DRAGON!" Before anyone could stop her, she scooped it up and hugged it tight—as though a dragon were some kind of doll! The dragon quickly folded its wings close to its body and tucked in its claws. I don't know why it didn't scratch her.

"Hey, don't squeeze it!" I warned. Rose looked at Philip, but he nodded, so she loosened her hold a bit. Even with her arms half hiding it, that dragon was something to look at: metallic green, but with blue in there too—the kind of shifting color that some hummingbirds and dragonflies are. Maybe whoever named dragonflies really knew about dragons. "Let me see it," I said.

"No," said Rose, "it's MINE!"

"Pets are always all of ours," I insisted. "Let me see it."

"PHILIP!" protested Rose.

"Not so loud," said Philip. "You'll wake up Mom and Dad. Anyway, Jason's right. If we're going to keep it, it belongs to all of us."

"But I HATCHED it," said Rose.

"It hatched itself," I said.

"Rose found it," decided Philip, "so she gets to name it. But it belongs to all of us." Bossy, as usual.

"Its name is Drag," said Rose, "because it is a dragon."

Trust Rose to give it a totally dumb name like that— but at least she finally did hand it over. I knew just how to hold it. Once it settled down, I stroked it under the chin, just on a chance—and it worked. The dragon tilted its head up, and slowly closed its amber eyes. It looked blissful.

"Is it a boy or a girl?" asked Rose.

Philip took that as his cue to grab it out of my hands. He looked. "I think a girl."

"I bet they won't let us keep her," I said. "Hey, look out, she's going to fall!" Drag was wriggling out of Philip's grasp. Before he could get a new grip, she escaped.

But she didn't fall. Spreading her wings, she glided

over to Rose's bed and made a perfect landing. "NEAT-O!" I said.

"She can fly!" said Rose.

"Well, of course," said The Voice of Authority. "She has wings." We were all staring at those wings. Stretched open in a patch of sunlight, they glinted with rainbow colors—like the surface of a soap bubble, like the wings of a dragonfly. They looked tough, but you could see light through them.

"Baby birds have wings too," I reminded Philip, "But THEY can't fly right away. Their parents have to bring them food for weeks."

I knew Philip was going to try to find some way to get in the last word on the subject, but we were all distracted by what Drag did next. As though she understood the word "food," she was turning from one of us to the other, her head raised, her mouth opened wide. There were plenty of teeth inside. She might be small, but she was definitely a dragon. "She's hungry!" Rose cried.

Philip frowned. "I'm not sure what to feed a dragon. In stories they eat maidens, but—"

"We can feed her Rose!" I suggested promptly. Rose made a face at me.

Philip ignored us and continued, "—but this one doesn't act fierce. Anyway, she's too little to eat anything live, except maybe a mouse."

"Let's wake up Mom and Dad," said Rose. "They'll

know what to feed her." Drag flew from the bed and landed on her shoulder, and Rose reached up to steady her there.

"We should keep her a secret," I reminded them. "I already told you—they probably won't let us keep her."

"Won't let you keep what?" said a sleepy voice. We looked around. Dad was coming down the hall, wrapping his robe around him.

"Uh oh," said Philip. "The cat's out of the bag."

Dad stared at Drag, who now was trying to lick Rose's hair smooth with a long green tongue. "THAT'S NO CAT!"

Chapter 2

Well, in a way I was right and in a way I was wrong. When I said they wouldn't let us keep her, I was thinking Mom and Dad would say we'd have to give Drag to a zoo or something. Actually, once the two of them got over the shock, the real problem was that they kept hogging Drag themselves. Mom especially. She was worse than Rose.

"Come on, sweet thing," she cooed, cuddling Drag close while trying to wedge some oatmeal into her mouth. Mom had found a slender spoon to use for the job, one left over from when Rose was a baby. "GOOD oatmeal." Drag turned her head to one side and shut her mouth tightly. I could see her eyes flash.

"She's a DRAGON, Mom," I protested.

"Try something with more protein," suggested Dad.

"Canned tuna, maybe?" said Mom.

"I'll get it," I said quickly. I didn't want anyone trying

to shove it down her throat with a baby spoon. I opened the can, dished about half of the tuna in a bowl and put the bowl in the middle of the table. Drag wriggled out of Mom's clutches, glided over and began to eat the tuna right away—daintily, like a cat.

"Oooh, look—she loves it." Mom was cooing again. "Just watch her eat. Those tiny little teeth! A real baby dragon. A dragon on our doorstep."

"Her egg wasn't on the doorstep," said Rose. "It was under a bush."

"That's just a way of saying she got left with us, and so we should take care of her," explained Philip. I waited for Mom or Dad to say well, but after all we couldn't really keep her—but they were wrapped up in watching Drag eat. None of our pets had ever been allowed up on the table. It looked as though the rules had changed, though. Dad just sat there ignoring his own breakfast, a silly grin on his face. "I can't believe it. A dragon."

"Then we get to keep her?" asked Philip.

Dad frowned. When he finally spoke, what he said wasn't at all what I had been expecting. "I'd say yes, if we can," he said, "at least for as long as we can. But we'll have to keep her a secret. They'll try to take her away if anyone finds out."

"Who'll take her away?" asked Rose.

Dad's mouth tightened. "SOMEONE," he said. "Scientists. Animal-rights people. Or maybe worse; I suppose some nut could decide she's really Satan in disguise and want to destroy her. Anyway, Someone. Someone who doesn't know any more about taking care of dragons than we do, but who wants to study her or make a cause around her or—" He hesitated, searching for words.

"—or something else stupid and grownup," I finished for him.

Mom gave me a look. "Your dad and I are grownups, and in case you haven't noticed we're with you on this one," she said. By that time Drag had finished eating her own food and was nibbling the bacon on Mom's plate. Mom didn't say boo. She just sat there running a finger over those glowing scales, watching the colors shift. Little by little, she started to smile. "Well after all, why shouldn't we keep her? There aren't any experts on dragons around now, if there ever were any. Anyone else trying to take care of her would just have to experiment, the way we will."

Drag sat up on her hind legs and touched her long tongue gently to Mom's cheek, almost as though she understood. Mom's smile broadened, and she rubbed Drag gently under the wings. "Anyway, I bet she'd be happier with us than in some cage at a university. I say we try it. If it starts to look as though we can't do a good job, then we turn her over to the Someones of the world."

Mom and Dad glanced quickly, almost shyly, at one another. They both looked sort of surprised, but I don't know whether it was because of what the other had said, or at their own words. The three of us took in that look and looked at each other in turn. I don't think any of us had thought they'd say yes. I hadn't really expected that we COULD just decide to keep her. I almost didn't have time to notice feeling happy, I was so amazed. But I probably was starting to grin. I know everyone else was.

Then Mom's smile faded, and she slowly rubbed the bridge of her nose. Uh oh, I thought. I held my breath, waiting for her to say whatever it was. DON'T HAVE SECOND THOUGHTS! I silently urged her. Finally she spoke. "Even if everything works," she said slowly, "we can't fool ourselves that we're getting a pet to keep. A dragon isn't designed as a house pet, and we can't make her into one. I expect the most we can do is try to keep her safe and healthy until she's ready to be on her own."

I didn't want to think that far ahead, and by the tone of her voice, she didn't either. But at least she wasn't changing her mind about keeping Drag for now. We nodded.

That started Dad thinking about the hard parts, too. His face grew serious. "You have to understand we won't be able to tell ANYONE," he said. "Mom and I won't; you kids won't. Not even our best friends. Because even if you think someone else can keep the secret, it will just be too much to expect. After all, a DRAGON."

"We can keep it secret," said Philip. "Don't worry."
Rose and I nodded.

As we talked, Drag was exploring the table. Now her tongue flicked out and back again, leaving a tiny nick in the cube of butter. She was motionless for a minute, then finally swallowed. You could see her thinking about whether to try a little more, but she must have decided it wasn't the right sort of food for dragons, because she went over instead to see what Rose had on her plate.

It was hard to do anything but watch Drag, but Mom pulled us back to the business of how to keep a dragon a secret. "It's not going to be simple," she reminded us. "She'll have to stay in the house, and that means you can't have your friends over any more, except to play in the yard."

"What do I tell them if they want to go to the bathroom?" asked Rose.

Mom bit her lip, thinking. "They know I do accounting work at home. Just tell them I've taken on a lot of new sets of books at once, and I'm so busy now that there has to be a new rule: NO kids inside. They'll just have to go home if they need the bathroom or a drink." We nodded.

"I'm not so much worried about kids as I am about Lady Long-ears next door," said Dad. "Better keep the shades down on that side of the house. She doesn't miss a trick."

"Our neighbor's name is Miss Binns, dear," said Mom, in her not-in-front-of-the-children voice. Then, in her regular voice, she added, "But I know what you mean. She's a wonderful librarian, but I think she missed a natural career as a detective. She knows EVERYTHING that goes on. But you can't criticize someone for having good hearing, or for being—well, remarkably observant."

Drag had slipped over to my place by that time and was letting me feed her bits of scrambled egg. She didn't seem to mind being fed as long as I just held things out in my fingers, letting her decide about whether or not to take them. At first I was a little nervous about those teeth—but she was careful to bite only the food, not my fingers. The eggs turned out to be a success; I could hardly hold out pieces for her quickly enough. Watching her gulp them down made me think about something else that could be a problem. "Another thing—the way Drag eats, she's going to get big FAST," I pointed out. "Right now she can fly around inside the house okay, but what happens when she gets bigger?"

Dad smiled. "One day at a time, kiddo. I suspect there are going to be lot of problems in taking her on, and we can put off working on that particular one for a little while."

"Maybe we could get a bigger house," suggested Rose.

Dad and Mom glanced at each other again, but this

time it was one of those looks that parents hope you won't catch. I caught it, though. "What's the matter?" I asked.

Mom looked uncomfortable. "Oh, nothing, nothing for sure. Just something that might come up and complicate things." She shrugged and gave a little half-smile. "But it's nothing to bother about now. As Dad says, one day at a time."

Philip spoke up. "I know we are just kids—" he started. Hah! When he talks in that voice you know he thinks he is as good as grown up already. He went on in this adult-to-adult tone, "—but since Drag is ours, too, if this might have something to do with keeping her I think you should tell us about it."

Dad nodded. "That's fair," he said. He paused, his face serious. "It's just something that MIGHT come up, the way Mom said. I learned last week that my company has started talking about transferring me to a new job. But the job wouldn't be here, or in some town where we could get a bigger house. It would be in the city, where we'd need to live in an apartment. Nothing is settled yet, though. It won't be settled for a while. It might not even happen."

"Is this new job one you'd like?" I asked.

Dad shrugged. "The salary would be good," he said. "A lot more than I make now. But it would be a desk job. I'd be a full-time administrator, in charge of getting the stuff I've been developing into production." He tapped the tips of his fingers together, staring gloomily at them. "I wouldn't get to tinker with things any more." He stared some more at his hands. "I'll take the transfer if I don't have a choice, but I can't say it's something I'd choose on my own."

"What would you do if you could do anything you wanted?" asked Rose. Drag was back with her now that my scrambled eggs were polished off. It looked now as though Rose were trying to get her to dance or something; she was holding Drag's front legs up and swaying her back and forth. Rose is too little to understand some things. Her stupid question proved it. If you work for a big company, you don't get to choose what you do.

Dad answered the question as though it were a sensible one. "Make kites," he said, smiling. "But I don't think I could earn a living doing that."

"One day at a time," repeated Mom firmly. She smiled, a real smile this time. "And TODAY we have a dragon in the family." She reached over and took Dad's hand. "So nothing is impossible, right?"

"Right," said Dad.

But Philip and I glanced quickly at one another. We weren't fooled. This transfer thing was something that Dad was really upset about—and of course a city apartment would be no place for a growing dragon. If it happened, it would be bad news.

When it came to that, I didn't think I wanted to

move to a big city myself. Still, nothing was sure yet. Anyway, we'd figure out something. Nothing was impossible.

Right?

Right.

Chapter 3

Those next weeks, when Drag was first settling in, were easy. As usual Rose was the lucky one. She wasn't old enough to go to school yet, so she had Drag to herself a lot. I can't believe some of the stuff Drag put up with. One day we came home and Rose had her all dressed up in doll clothes—slits cut in the sides so the doll dress could slide over the wings. I couldn't believe Drag let her do it. If I had been a dragon, I would have bitten her.

But when Philip and I were there, Rose knew better than to try that stuff. And once we were home, we made sure Drag got enough exercise to make up for all the coddling. Usually we played with Drag in the living room, pushing all the lamps next to the walls so they wouldn't get knocked over. Our favorite game was one I thought of, beanbag keep-away. We used a beanbag because it was easier for Rose and Drag to catch than a ball. Mom had thought Drag's teeth might tear the beanbag, but they didn't. Dad said Drag had a gentle mouth, like those dogs that retrieve game birds without mussing a feather.

Anyway, we'd race around throwing the beanbag to one another, and Drag would try to snag it in midair. You could tell she loved it. Sometimes she would come flying to us with the beanbag in her mouth, begging us to play. Playing keep-away was fun for us too, but the real reason we loved the game was because it was so great watching her fly. Drag was a moving jewel, a flash of iridescent green. She kept reminding me of hummingbirds and dragonflies—not just because of her colors, but because she was an acrobat in the air the way they are. She could beat her wings and keep in one place, and then suddenly SWOOP, she had the beanbag between her jaws.

While I was at school I could hardly wait for the last bell to ring. Even when I wasn't actually thinking about Drag, I always had this feeling that there was something special waiting for me. It was like the feeling you get when you wake up on your birthday, even before you remember what day it is.

So during those first weeks, I tried not to wonder about the fact that Dad seemed to be getting more and more quiet. At least he didn't say anything more about that job transfer—and I didn't ask. Once in a while, though, I'd catch a look on his face that made me pretty sure the possibility was still there to worry him. When that happened, all I could do was tell myself to forget it. At least it still wasn't anything sure. Even if we did have to move, we'd figure out some way to keep Drag. Yeah—one day at a time, I told myself. And each day was different, because Drag was changing each day. You could almost see her grow. Mom had discovered that she really liked canned dog- and cat-food and that made feeding her easy.

Before long, Drag was bigger than a large cat—and that's not counting her wings. About that time I noticed we began to win more at keep-away. "Drag is having a hard time keeping from bumping into the walls," I finally pointed out to the other two. "I'm not sure the game is fair any more. She needs more room."

"Maybe Mom and Dad can help us sneak her out to where there aren't any people," suggested Rose, "so she can really fly."

"I already asked Dad about that," said Philip, in his Voice of Authority. "There aren't any places safe enough. It's too open out where the farms are. Even in the woods there are sometimes hikers, and everywhere there are planes flying overhead. Someone would see her."

I couldn't argue with that. But more and more, I found myself wishing that we could take her outside. When Drag flew through shafts of sunlight coming in the window, you could imagine how those metallic scales would look out in the open, on a sunny day.

Still, that seemed the closest thing to a problem that we had. But then one Wednesday Drag didn't finish her dinner. She ate part of it and then glided quietly off to a corner and curled up. "Have you kids been feeding Drag snacks?" said Mom. "I don't want her getting a lot of junk food."

We all said no. I could tell by Mom's look she wasn't sure whether or not to believe us. But I knew I hadn't fed her anything, and I was pretty sure Rose and Philip hadn't either. I shoveled my own dinner down as quickly as I could, excused myself from the table, and went over to take a look at Drag. She had acted okay that afternoon, but it wasn't like her to take a nap right after dinner. I couldn't see anything wrong with her, though. When I tickled her under the chin she opened her eyes and her tongue flicked out to give my hand a touch. "She's probably just tired," I said.

I tried to tell myself the same thing that night, and finally I managed to fall asleep.

The next day, though, Drag only picked at her breakfast. I had a hard time concentrating on school work that day. In the afternoon when Philip and I got back, Rose was waiting for us on the front lawn. Her face looked as if she had been crying. Usually that doesn't mean much; Rose cries about anything. But this day when she ran to meet us looking like that, we speeded up to get to her fast.

"I think she's sick," Rose whimpered. "Come see. She isn't just acting funny; she doesn't look right."

"Be quiet," hissed Philip. He jerked his head toward Miss Binns. We were right in front of her house, and she was there in her front yard with some friend of hers. Philip stepped close to Rose. "That was stupid," he whispered.

Philip is almost never cross with Rose. I was afraid she would start blubbering, but she only hissed back, "I never SAID. . . ."

"Fight some other time," I muttered to them. We hurried inside together and into Rose's room. Drag was on the bed.

Philip pushed me aside, of course, to get the first look. "She looks pretty normal to me," he said, after inspecting her.

"That's what Mom said—but see, her scales look different," insisted Rose. "They're more yellow than they used to be, and they're getting kind of cloudy-looking." By that time I was around on the other side of the bed, trying to get a look myself. Once Rose said that, I thought I could see what she meant—but I wasn't sure.

"It's your imagination," said Philip firmly, the good old Voice of Authority. "It's the light in here. You're just worried because she hasn't been eating. Come on, Jason. I bet she just needs some exercise. That will fix her appetite."

Drag flew down the hall after us into the living

room, her wing tips barely missing the walls. She WAS getting big, I realized. But once there, she just landed on the couch and lay down. We coaxed her and coaxed her, tossing the beanbag in the air. Philip and I even tried standing at opposite ends of the couch and throwing it back and forth right over her head, while Rose bounced the cushions up and down to get her going. Nothing we could think of could get Drag to open her wings again. After a while she sighed, closed her eyes and curled into a ball.

And when dinnertime came Drag didn't touch her food at all. By this time, of course, she was using a dish on the floor—she was definitely too big for us to let her eat on the table any more. But that night Mom tried lifting her up onto her lap, cuddling her the way she had the day she hatched, and offering her bites of meat loaf. No luck.

I suddenly didn't feel like finishing my own dinner.

After we cleared off our plates, Mom turned up the light above the dining-room table as bright as it would go and lifted Drag onto the table so she could get a good look at her. "You know, I guess Rose was right after all," she admitted. "Her scales definitely are more yellow now, and they don't shine any more."

Dad leaned over Drag too. "And her eyes," he said. "They ARE cloudy."

"I don't think she can see so well any more," I told him. I turned to Philip. "I bet one reason she doesn't want to fly around now is because she might bump into things."

By that time nobody wanted dessert. We moved into the living room for a family conference.

"I know we thought we could take care of her," said Mom, "but maybe it's time to call in a vet."

"I'm scared," said Rose. "Mom, is Drag going to die?"

Mom hugged Rose closer to her, but all she answered was, "I don't think we need to worry about that right now." I could tell Mom was trying to make her voice sound comforting—but if you thought about what she actually said, it wasn't one hundred percent reassuring.

"I guess it's not fair to keep her if we don't know how to help her," said Philip slowly.

I turned to Mom. "You said there aren't any experts on dragons," I reminded her. "How would a vet know what to do? At least we know Drag; we've had some experience with her. That should help some. That should count."

I knew perfectly well that none of us wanted to let Drag go. I certainly didn't want to hand her over to Someone. Not to anyone. I thought hard, searching for some way out. The best I could come up with seemed pretty feeble, but I tried it. I turned to Dad. "You always tell us that if we need to learn something new," I reminded him, "the library will probably have books to tell us what we need to know. Wouldn't there be something in the library about what might be wrong with her?"

To my surprise, Dad's face lit up, and he gave my shoulder a squeeze. "Worth a try!" he said. "Look, let's try that before we go for anything more drastic. The library's open until nine. I'll go down and check out everything that might give us a clue as to what is wrong. Not the books with dragons in them—those are just fiction—but books on every kind of animal that might possibly be related to dragons. Lizards, dinosaurs, alligators, snakes, everything like that."

He looked at each of us to make sure we all understood. The excitement on his face, the energy in his voice, made me feel better—not just about Drag, but about him too. Suddenly he was looking and sounding like the old Dad. "The rest of you get some sleep tonight. I promise I'll do a crash course on the medical problems of any animal even vaguely like a dragon. If by morning I can't figure out what's wrong, then at breakfast we can talk about whether we should call in a vet or the biology department at the university or the reptile house at the zoo or whatever. Okay?"

We all looked over at Drag, who was curled up on the couch next to Mom and Rose. She looked sleepy. At least she didn't look as though anything hurt; that was reassuring. "I think that's a good plan," said Mom.

"It leaves the rest of us out," I protested. "I bet

there'll be a lot of books. You probably couldn't go through them all if you stayed up all night! Philip and I are good readers. We can help, and so can Mom."

"Well, of course, I'll help, but I'm afraid that on a school night—" Mom began, but Dad touched her hand.

"Jason's right," he said. "We all should be in on it. If Rose could read, I'd say let her stay up too." He gave each of us a quick hug, patted Drag, and rushed out to the car.

We didn't talk much after he left. Rose lay snuggling Drag on the couch until it was her bedtime. At almost nine, Dad still wasn't back. Mom took longer than usual to tuck Rose in, I guess trying to get her to stop worrying. She had just returned to the living room when Dad came in the front door with a stack of books so tall he was having trouble balancing it. "Let's get to work," he said.

We settled around the table. Philip pulled out the books on dinosaurs and put them in a stack in front of him. "I thought you knew everything about dinosaurs already," I reminded him, but right away I wished I hadn't; this was no time to needle him. But he just ignored me.

The rest of us simply took the nearest book and started in. My first book was on turtles. Even though it was pretty thick, it didn't take me as much time to go through it as I had expected. I didn't really have to read the whole thing. I just checked the index to see if there were any special sections on turtle diseases—which there weren't—and then skimmed the pages, making sure something about what made turtles sick wasn't mentioned in passing.

Nothing. I reached for the next one. Lizards, this time.

When the hall clock chimed eleven, Mom looked up. "Sure you boys aren't getting sleepy? Dad and I can finish."

Philip's eyes looked ready to close, but like me he shook his head. I didn't feel sleepy at all; I was too worried. We had gone through a lot of the books already but so far no clue. I didn't want to think about what would happen if none of the books helped.

Chapter

4

It was after midnight when I found the answer; it was in a book about snakes. There had been nothing about snake diseases in the index, but I was scanning the pages, just to be sure. I was so tired by then that I had to read the paragraph twice, to be certain I wasn't dreaming that what it said connected with what we were worrying about. Then I read it a third time carefully. Suddenly I didn't feel tired at all. I lifted my head and announced triumphantly, "It's okay! She's not even sick!"

The other three looked up. They looked doubtful, but I grinned. It was hard not to feel smug. Finding the answer was a lot harder than finding the egg, and I had recognized that what I read was the answer. Someone else might have missed it. "I'm pretty sure. She's just shedding, like a snake."

"Shedding?" said Mom blankly. She was the one

who looked sleepy.

Right away The Voice of Authority had to take over, as though Mom were a baby like Rose. "You know how when snakes get too big for their skins they grow a new skin under the old, tight one, and then they just wriggle out and leave the old skin behind."

"That's why her eyes are getting cloudy, why she's having trouble seeing," I told him. "The thin membrane that protected her eyes has separated already. Now it's just in the way of the new one, like a pair of cloudy glasses. And that's why her scales are getting all dull-looking. Once she sheds the old skin, everything should be all right." I passed the book around, and they all read the part about shedding.

"Why is she getting yellow?" asked Philip. "The book doesn't say anything about that."

"I don't know," I admitted. "Maybe the color change is something that just happens with dragons. The rest of what is going on is just like what happens with snakes, though."

But his question made me feel less certain. Drag was still sleeping on the couch. I went in and ran my fingertip along her dry, scaly skin, pulling at it a little. Yes, it did feel tight. I noticed for the first time that I could see little spaces of skin now between the scales; I was sure they hadn't always been there. Of course. She had been growing and growing, and the scales had been pulling farther apart. Now the skin had stretched until the edges of the scales weren't even touching. It just couldn't stretch any more. Seeing those spaces, feeling the tight skin, made me feel okay again. I returned to the dining room and suddenly realized I was hungry. "How about a midnight snack? It's midnight and then some."

"Heavens, we never had dessert!" exclaimed Mom. We cleared the books off the table and started in on the brownies and milk she brought us. I couldn't remember anything ever tasting so good.

"How long will it take her to shed?" I asked as I munched. "Does it hurt? The book didn't say anything about that."

"I don't know," said Dad, "I guess it could take a while. I shouldn't think it would hurt. The book made it sound as though snakes take shedding in stride. I expect it's the same with dragons." I had to be content with that.

It was early Friday morning now. We all agreed that we'd give Drag through the weekend to shed, before we even started thinking again about taking her to Someone. I wasn't worried about that any more; I was pretty sure my answer was the right one. The only thing I was worrying about was how I was going to stay awake in school that day.

Well, there's no way I can ever be sure, but after watching Drag do it the first time I decided shedding an old skin might actually be fun—the way that peeling off dead skin after a sunburn is. It went a lot faster, though.

Peeling can go on for days. Once Drag started to get the old skin off, it only took a few hours.

That same afternoon Rose came running out to meet us again, looking all excited and started pulling us into the house. The three of us automatically looked toward Miss Binn's house as we ran up the walk, but there was no sign of her in the yard. This time Rose was smart enough not to say anything not until we were inside. Then she burst out, "It's happening! She's been rubbing and rubbing on the couch, and she's got her whole head out!"

We saw immediately what Rose meant. The brilliant new scales of Drag's head and neck rose from a ring of dull folds. It looked almost as though her head were emerging from a yellowish turtleneck sweater. The top part, the opening for that gleaming neck, was the edge of the old skin that once had bordered her long mouth. Now Drag was rolling back and forth, twisting and turning, rubbing first her back and then her stomach against the rough weave of the couch. I could tell the old skin was loosening. Between the scales, the membrane of skin was almost transparent. I could see the new scales sliding underneath, watch the old skin slipping a little over the new.

But I didn't see how she could possibly squeeze her whole body through that narrow part that was around the neck! Exactly as though she had read my thought, Drag stopped wriggling, sat up and hooked one sharp claw over the edge of the turtleneck of old skin. She began sawing with the claw, the same way she had sawed though the shell of her egg when she was little—cutting a slit through the tough membrane between the old scales. When the slit was finished, it ran diagonally clear down to where her right wing started.

"Hey, look; the skin doesn't cover the wings," said Philip, leaning over her. "She's getting her wings free." The Voice of Authority always had to announce the obvious. By this time Drag had switched claws and was working on a second slit, this one on the left side.

Up to then Mom had been ducking in and out, keeping an eye on progress but still pretending she was working on those ledger books she does at home. When it got to this point, though, she couldn't stay away; she watched the whole last part along with us.

Getting this far had kept Drag working hard, but now things got easier. With all that rubbing and twisting, the old skin was pretty well detached. The minute the second slit was finished, a whole big flap just folded down all by itself, exposing the handsome new scales on Drag's chest. From then on, it was a piece of cake —just a question of wiggling out of the rest of the skin. Getting the feet out seemed to be the only part that was hard at all. We watched as Drag struggled to free one foot, looking as though she were trying to pull a hand out of a tight glove. "Maybe we could help her," I suggested.

30

"We shouldn't," said Philip firmly. "Suppose the old skin there isn't all loose yet? We might yank off some of the new scales." Mom nodded. Well, even I had to see he could be right, and of course Rose always agrees with anything Philip says, so we stayed out of it. Drag finally resorted to using her teeth to help with that foot. The old skin did get one tiny rip, but the new scales weren't even scratched.

Drag had to saw one more slit, so that the hard, rubbery spade-thing on the end of her tail could slip out with the rest of it. "Look, that part of her tail is like the wings," said Philip. "It isn't covered with scales." Maybe Philip will earn a fortune some day as a TV sports announcer, I thought, telling the audience what's happening even when everyone can see it for himself.

Anyway, once the tip of her tail was out Drag stepped away from the old skin, shook herself, stretched up on her hind legs, and spread her wings as if to say, "Look at me now!" It was all over before Dad was even back from work. It didn't seem fair that he missed the whole thing. "At least," said Mom, "we can lay out the old skin on the rug to show him. But the membrane between scales is awfully thin. It may already be starting to dry out and get fragile. Let's lift it together, to be sure it doesn't tear." We all slid our hands under the yellowish skin. Mom supported the middle part, Philip the part that had covered the head, I took care of the legs, and Rose was in charge of the tail. "Gently," Mom cautioned. "All the same time. One, two, three, LIFT. My goodness, these scales are heavier than I would have expected!"

I was thinking the same thing. The connecting skin couldn't have weighed more than thick plastic wrap would have, so it must have been the scales themselves that made it so heavy. "Drag must have been happy to get that skin off," I agreed. "She's been carrying around two sets of scales at once. They must have weighed a ton." It was weird, the skin being so heavy. Drag hadn't felt all that heavy, sitting on our laps.

Chapter 5

We got the old skin all neatly arranged, and stood back to admire the contrast between Drag's first set of scales and our gleaming dragon. Drag lolled on the couch, preening herself. She flicked the tip of her tongue over her new scales to check them out, and rubbed her head against them as if she were polishing them.

"The skin looks smaller than Drag," said Rose.

I snickered. "A tight girdle that a fat lady has finally managed to wriggle out of."

"Drag's not fat!" protested Rose.

"Jason, you don't always have to say things you think will annoy Rose," said Philip.

"Philip, you don't always have to tell Jason what to do," I said, in exactly the same voice he had used.

Mom sighed.

Fortunately, just then Dad came in from work.

"LOOK!" all four of us said at once.

Dad stared at the skin on the floor. "Already?" he exclaimed. "I thought it would take days! And she didn't wait for me!" He shook his head at Drag, who was arching her neck over an uplifted front foot, checking out the polish. "Hey, the old girl's looking pretty proud of herself."

"Can I have the old skin?" asked Rose.

"You can't ever show it to anyone," I said. "What would you do with it?"

"I'd keep it," said Rose. "So when I'm grown up I can remember Drag when she was little."

Rose goes in for soupy stuff like that. I just shrugged. Philip said, "Fine with me, she can have it."

"This won't be the last time Drag sheds," Mom told Rose. "If you're going to want to keep all her skins, I suppose we can make room at the back of your closet for the collection. But we'll need a pretty big carton." She went off to find a box.

That night's dinner felt like a party. I had to open three whole cans of food for Drag before she seemed full—she had never eaten so much at one time before. "This dragon is going to eat us out of house and home," said Mom—but she sounded happy about it.

"I'd say her days of flying around the living room are clearly numbered," said Dad. "I guess we have to begin facing it now; she is going to be BIG. Fortunately..." He cleared his throat in a proud way, making sure he had our attention. "Fortunately, I have a plan ready for the next stage. It's a little risky, but we have to do something. We can't keep her cooped up much longer."

"A plan?" said Mom. So this was new to her, too.

Dad grinned. Maybe his plan was risky, but he didn't look worried—he looked excited. "Well, it will take a while to explain," he said. "For starters, unless it turns out that someone has a better plan than mine, we're going to have to keep both cars on the street from now on."

Mom's face went carefully blank; I could tell she was trying not to look disappointed. "I know we have a three-car garage," she said gently, "but at the rate Drag seems to be growing, even the garage isn't going to give her the room she'll need for too long. I'm afraid we won't be buying very much time by moving her out there."

Dad's grin broadened. "My idea is a little more complicated than just moving Drag to the garage," he said. "Something Rose asked helped give me the idea. Let me tell you about it, okay?"

And he did.

Well, the plan wasn't really all that complicated, it had to do with an act we were going to put on, but of course we had to explain it to Rose more than once. Philip did most of the explaining, and before long it was sounding as though he had thought it up in the first place. Once everybody understood what Dad had in mind, we all had ideas to add to it. I was the one who suggested that Flash could help us get things done faster. "He'll probably guess right off that we aren't telling him the whole truth," Mom objected. We finally convinced her it was worth the extra risk. Philip as usual kept wanting to get every little nit-picky detail perfectly defined, so it was Rose's bedtime before everyone was satisfied that we had everything thought through. Dad called Flash the minute our conference broke up and scheduled things to start at nine o'clock the next morning.

After Philip and I were finally in our bunks that night, I kept going over in my mind what we were going to try. It sounded exciting, it sounded like fun, but Dad was right—it sounded risky. "Do you think it will really work?" I asked Philip softly.

He was so long in answering me that at first I thought he had already managed to fall asleep. But for once he hadn't. At last his answer came from the darkness above my head. "It has to. I can't think of anything better." Quite an admission, from him.

Chapter

6

There wasn't much that we kids could do to help that first weekend, but we still hung around the garage watching most of the time. We always hung around when Flash was there.

Flash takes some explaining, and I might as well do that right now.

Flash had only lived in our neighborhood about a year. I still remember Mom's face the first time she saw him rev up his Harley-Davidson and VAROOM by. That day Flash was wearing his favorite leather jacket with the initials "BB" in silver studs on the back, the first "B" facing backwards. There were fancy designs in silver paint all around the initials. As he passed I glimpsed a tattoo on one of his hands. His bushy black beard had a lot of grey in it; there was a red bandanna tied around his head. If old pirates rode motorcycles and wore leather jackets, they might look a lot like Flash. Mom had been talking over the fence to Miss Binns. As the roar of the motorcycle faded in the distance she just stood there, her head gradually swiveling between where the motorcycle had turned the corner and the house down the street from which Flash had emerged.

Most people in that neighborhood were pretty ordinary. Whatever you could say about the way Flash looked, it wasn't ordinary.

"He's a new neighbor?" Mom finally asked.

"Why, yes," said Miss Binns. "He came in for a library card just last week. He seems to be a great reader, actually. We had a most interesting conversation. His name is Mr. Martin, although he apparently prefers to be addressed by a nickname. I'm aware it's somewhat old-fashioned of me to prefer addressing people more formally, so I was pleased when he was quite understanding about it."

My mother was still looking dazed, so Miss Binns continued, scarcely pausing for breath. "I gather he has recently retired from driving long-distance trucks, although he has done many other things as well, some of them quite colorful. That striking jacket is a memento of his membership in a motorcycle gang, some years back. Not one of those vicious gangs, I'm glad to say."

". . .BB?"

"When I asked him about the initials, he said they stood for Brothers of Beelzebub. I was concerned that the name had a sinister ring. But Mr. Martin explained to me the group was actually nothing at all like the Hell's Angels." Miss Binns shook her head, smiling gently. "Grownup little boys, some of these groups. I expect they were hoping to shock people with such a name." Her expression grew more serious. "I gather there was considerable drinking, however. To Mr. Martin's credit, that struck him as an unwise habit in a group dedicated to riding a powerful but most unprotected vehicle, and he assured me he did not share in the custom. In any case, he ended his association with the club about fifteen years ago, at the time he began driving heavy trucks for a living. I think he had rather outgrown the group by that time."

It is really amazing what Miss Binns can find out from someone applying for a library card.

Mom blinked, digesting all this. "So now he is simply . . . enjoying a quiet retirement?"

"Yes, although I gather he finds inactivity to be tedious," responded Miss Binns. "He asked if he might post a notice on the library bulletin board offering his services as a handyman. I explained that we could not accept personal advertisements of that sort on our board but promised that I would mention his availability to my acquaintances. In spite of his unorthodox appearance, he seems to be quite skilled in many practical fields. I myself called him in two days ago about a persistent leak in the kitchen wall, one that my regular plumber had been unable to fix to my satisfaction. Mr.

Martin had the problem correctly diagnosed in no time; he repaired it most skillfully. His charge was quite reasonable."

Mom repeated this whole conversation pretty much word for word to Dad at dinner. All those details broke him up. "She didn't tell you his shoe size?" he guffawed. "I bet she found it out!" When he stopped laughing, he said, "Look, I want to meet this guy. Promise me you'll give him a call next time something needs fixing, even if you think I might be able to do it. And have him come on the weekend, when I can be home." Mom gave him her are-you-serious look. "I MEAN it," said Dad. "Look, if Lady Long-ears trusts him in her kitchen, he certainly can't be a dangerous character—and face it, how many interesting ones do we have around here? I mean it; I want a chance to see him in action."

It turned out Miss Binns was right; Flash was a wizard handyman. But what we kids liked was that while he worked he would tell about all the things he had done in his life. Some of them were pretty amazing. And I liked the way he listened to my own stories—really listened, so that it made me feel like an interesting character too.

He and Dad hit it off right away. At first Mom complained that she wasn't sure Flash knew the difference between the things he had really done and things he had only read about, between the places he had been and places he only knew from books. Before long, though, I think she decided it didn't matter.

One thing about Flash was sure: he never said he knew how to do something unless he did. So far, we actually hadn't found very much he didn't know how to do. So the only reason Mom had for hesitating to let him help with our plan was that she thought he might guess what was really up. But that was just one of the risks in the plan, after all. She knew Flash would be a big help.

Chapter
7

So anyway, there was Flash in the garage that Saturday morning, starting out by helping Dad stow anything that we didn't really use up into the rafters. Next they figured out how to hang the stuff we use in the yard somewhere along the far wall. Once the garage was clear, the two of them started unloading lumber from Flash's big van, the one he uses when he has to carry things that won't fit on a motorcycle. As they worked, Dad was explaining why he wanted to turn the garage into a workshop.

"You been thinking about trying this a long time?" Flash asked Dad as he set up his sawhorses and got out his electric saw.

"On and off," answered Dad. "I've always liked inventing things—that's one of the things that got me into my present line of work. But when I was young, it was never anything practical, just stuff I liked making for fun. And kites were what I liked making most of all. I decided back then that if I could make kites that were special enough, I could sell the designs to some big company and make a fortune."

"So why haven't you already ended up as a world-famous kite designer?" asked Flash, measuring the wall that was going to have the workbench running along it. "Turn out to be hard inventing ones that were special enough?"

"Actually, no," answered Dad, carrying the two-by-fours over and stacking them next to the sawhorses. "Believe me, that's the part I was good at. You should have seen some of them. Peacocks with wings that flapped, phoenixes with tails that looked like real flames. I made special kites to fly at night, round ones that looked like glowing moons trailing stars in their wake. I could even make kites that looked as though they were changing shape and color as they flew."

"So why didn't it work out? What went wrong?" asked Flash, measuring the lumber for the supports.

"Well, I was still green behind the ears, back then," said Dad. "I never could find a company I could get interested in making my kites, and I didn't know any other way to get started." He shrugged. "And then I started inventing other things, practical things that companies knew they needed. Those ideas were easy to sell. After a while I decided I had to let the kites go."

Flash's saw bit into the wood, and it was too noisy

to talk for a while. But he must have kept on thinking about what Dad had said. As he started to assemble the workbench base, he asked, "And so now you finally know how to sell kite designs?"

Dad shrugged. "I know a lot more now about how the world works, at least. I shouldn't have wasted my time trying to interest ordinary companies in making superkites. For something special like that, you really need to start a company of your own. I couldn't have done it back then, even if I had known enough to try— but now I have more contacts. I maybe can find backers. It wouldn't take that much capital, after all. We're not talking about mass-production kites here. No huge factory to build. These would be mostly hand-crafted."

Flash measured and cut the last braces for the workbench. "Could a small business like that make a real profit?"

Dad hesitated. As he and Flash carried the cut lumber into the garage, he finally answered. "I think so. The materials wouldn't cost that much. The designs aren't really all that complicated to make. If anything is good enough, people will pay through the nose for it. You've seen those glossy catalogs from fancy stores, the prices they charge?" Flash nodded, so Dad continued, "I think we could get prices like that. A kite can be more than a toy. A really great kite has some magic to it." He stopped talking for a minute, looking off into space. I guess he was remembering those kites he made, back before we were born. "Anyway, the first step is to make some demonstration models. They can prove to potential investors that I've got some magic to sell. I figure it's worth a try."

Flash was assembling the supports for the workbench—making everything look easy, the way he always does. As the base began to take shape, Dad started to haul the sheets of plywood for the top over to the sawhorses.

"You know," Flash called back to Dad, "I'm good for more than just this kind of rough carpentry. I apprenticed more than a year with a cabinet-maker once. And I have to admit, I've always had a thing for kites myself. You want any help making these models, I'd do it on my own time. And listen, if this project gets off the ground and you want an assistant or whatever—well, keep me in mind."

"Flash, if we get it that far, you're on," responded Dad. "Can't think of anyone I'd rather work with."

Flash was crouched low, fastening the last supports together with long screws. The day was hot, and his sleeveless red T-shirt was soaked with sweat. He straightened, pulled off the shirt, draped it on the end of a rake that hung on the other wall and went back to work.

Dad was carrying the last sheet of plywood over to the sawhorses. He had been listening to Flash, not watching him. But when Flash stripped off that T-shirt, the three of us kids stood there staring. Then Rose ran over to Dad, grabbed his arm and silently pointed.

You know, I certainly would never want to get tattooed myself. Most of the time, I think tattoos are a stupid idea—but on Flash they were okay. All of us knew the tattoos on Flash's arms and hands: the American flag, the hula dancer that swayed when he flexed his muscles, the "MOM" in a banner below a heart, the fancy designs across his knuckles. They were part of Flash, so they weren't stupid.

But none of us had known that he had his biggest and most elaborate tattoo on his back. It was a dragon. And even though the colors weren't exactly right, the dragon looked a whole lot like Drag.

Dad looked at the tattoo, blinked, swallowed, then put his lips firmly together and held his finger to them. We understood. We wouldn't say anything, we wouldn't ask anything. And we certainly wouldn't tell Flash the colors weren't quite right. Flash was no dummy. He'd ask, "How do you know?"—and even if we didn't tell him the answer, he might guess.

So we just stood there, watching the dragon on Flash's back move a little as he finished setting those last screws. Maybe Mom had been right in worrying that Flash would be more likely than most people to guess what we were really up to. But I didn't feel worried, exactly. It just seemed funny he had that particular tattoo and that we hadn't known about it.

46

And then I began to think about something else: about what Dad had been telling Flash and how his voice had sounded when he told it. Maybe we didn't want Flash to know what we were really up to—but I began to wonder if I myself were sure about what that was. I had thought I understood the kite-building thing was just a front, but now I wasn't sure.

It didn't seem much use talking to Philip about what was confusing me. Philip knows plenty of facts, but not a whole lot about people. And Rose is too little to understand anything complicated. So I went inside to find Mom.

Chapter 8

Mom was working on one of those ledger books she does stuff with, but she stopped right away when I came in the den. "What's up, Jason?" she asked quietly.

I sometimes wish she couldn't guess so easily when something is bothering me, but at least I didn't have to beat around the bush.

"We're going to make some fancy kites, and let people know we are going to be testing them, right?"

"Right."

"And we'll say the tests have to be private, because we're planning to start a new business, and the designs need to be kept secret, at least until we get them just right and have them patented. Right?"

"Right."

"But we'll make sure people just happen to see one or two kites in action, so word will get around that Dad knows how to make kites that look real, kites that do things, kites that are almost magic. That way we can take Drag out in the country and let her fly while the kites are up. If someone sees her flying, we can say it was one of the kites. Right?"

"Right."

"Okay. Now what I want to know is—is this kite business really just pretend, so that we can have a safe way to let Drag fly outside? Or is Dad really going to start making kites for a living?"

Mom hesitated.

I had more questions, so I kept going. "Does this have anything to do with that stuff about maybe moving? You remember, that transfer that Dad talked about, back when we first got Drag?" She still didn't answer, so I got in my last question. "Is Dad going to try this for real so that we won't have to move, no matter what his company decides?"

"Oh, Jason," said Mom. "I wish there were always good answers to perfectly good questions." She put down her pen and swiveled her chair so she was facing me. "All I can do is tell you what I think. Well, I think that if we asked him, Dad would say that this whole thing is pretend. That it's just a cover to let Drag fly the way she needs to fly, to build strength in her wings, without people finding out about her." She shrugged and gestured toward the garage. "But I guess you've noticed he's as happy as a clam out there with Flash. I haven't seen him this happy in a long time. And I do know he always has thought about starting a kite business. I've known that for years. Not a definite plan, exactly, just a dream of something he'd like to try again, someday when he could." She paused again, pushed her chair back, and stood up. "If there were some way he could earn a living by designing and making the best kites in the world, he'd do it in a minute. And you know, I think there's a good chance the idea might even work."

I felt even more confused now, but I could tell she wasn't finished, so I waited. Mom gave me a quick hug, sighed, walked over to the window that let her see the garage, and shook her head. "But even small businesses take money to get started. I'm afraid that the part that makes it just pretend is that there's no way we could get that much money together. A venture like this is too risky to appeal to the kind of businessmen Dad knows, and heaven knows we don't have the money ourselves. I wouldn't feel safe about trying to borrow that much, even if I thought a bank would lend it to us. Which I don't."

"So then it is really just pretend?"

Mom came away from the window and gave me another hug. "I think so. But I'm afraid that without admitting it to himself, Dad may be starting to hope that once word gets around that he can make these great kites, an investor will appear from somewhere. I think he's starting to hope someone will really put up the money he needs to start the business, and it can all come true. If that magic investor doesn't appear, Dad could end up pretty disappointed. And then if later on it turns out he has to accept that transfer, well—having had these hopes will make the move that much harder on him. Once you start to believe in a dream, it's hard to let it go."

I didn't know what to say. I certainly didn't see how to make Dad stop hoping or Mom stop worrying about him. But anyway, now I understood how it was. It makes me feel better to understand things.

Just then the doorbell rang.

"Hey, maybe it's a magic investor!" I said.

Mom wasn't in a mood to joke. "Check to make sure Drag is in one of the bedrooms and that the door is closed," she ordered. "I'll go answer the bell."

Drag was asleep on Rose's bed, so all I had to do was close the door quietly, making sure the latch had caught. Then I started back down the hall toward the living room—but stopped when I heard Miss Binns' voice.

"I'm glad I caught you alone, my dear," she was saying. "I have been feeling for some time we should have a frank talk, and when I saw the children with your husband and Mr. Martin in the garage I thought this might be the ideal moment."

It didn't seem the ideal moment to let her know I wasn't in the garage any more, but I didn't know where

I could go—so I sat down on the hall carpet. I didn't think Mom would blame me for listening, and I was willing to bet that in my place it's exactly what Miss Binns would have done.

"I felt I had to let you know of the unfortunate gossip," said Miss Binns, "because I fear that unless the matter is cleared up soon your children's social life may suffer. Although of course it is already somewhat limited by your new circumstances."

"New circumstances?" asked Mom cautiously. "Gossip?"

"The ironic thing," continued Miss Binns, ignoring her, "is that my own understanding of your situation and the mistaken notion behind the gossip arose simultaneously. Both my enlightenment and those lamentable rumors, that is to say, were initiated by the very same incident."

"I'm not sure I understand," said Mom. "What rumors?"

This time Miss Binns acknowledged her question. "Why, the ridiculous idea that you have taken to drink," she said in a kindly tone.

"TAKEN TO DRINK?" said my mother, her voice no longer under control.

"Oh dear, I knew this would upset you. I haven't been explaining things at all clearly. Come, let's sit down." I could picture Miss Binns settling herself neatly on the couch, my mother sinking into a chair facing her. "Well, it started that day when I was giving Mrs. Throckhurst advice on what to do about the aphids on her calendulas. We both happened to overhear Rose's artless remark. It caught our attention, you see, because the child was so distraught."

"What did Rose say?" asked Mom weakly.

"Her words were, if memory serves, 'I think she's sick. Come see. She isn't just acting funny; she doesn't look right.' Your boys, on hearing these words, appeared to try to shush her, and then all three rushed indoors. Mrs. Throckhurst, of course, believed that you must be the only one home and assumed the child was referring to you."

"Oh," said Mom.

"And I fear," continued Miss Binns calmly, "that she put this incident together with the fact that in the weeks preceding, your children had prevented their little playmates from entering the house. The excuse that you had undertaken unusual amounts of bookkeeping responsibility she regarded as mere pretext. She assumed that your children were aware of a problem with alcohol and endeavored to shield the family from exposure of it to the world."

"I see," murmured Mom, without any great conviction.

"Mrs. Throckhurst had, it happens, encountered you at the market that very morning," Miss Binns went on. "She saw you there again the succeeding morning; you appeared to be in perfect health both times. So she rejected the possibility that it was some physical illness from which you suffered that was distressing little Rose."

"Oh," said Mom.

"It was perhaps fortunate," added Miss Binns, "that this incident took place on a Thursday."

"A Thursday?" Mom echoed.

"Well, on other weekdays I work my regular shift at the library. But on Thursdays, I have been trading my afternoon hours for Mrs. Garretson's evening ones, so that she may attend a ceramics class. I was therefore in my garden on that Thursday afternoon and able to observe for myself what Mrs. Throckhurst later recounted to others with such unfortunate embroideries." Miss Binns paused, as if offering Mom a chance to comment. "And of course I was in the library later that same evening, when your husband came rushing in, obviously upset."

"I see," said my mother slowly. This time she sounded as though she were beginning to mean it.

"Now, if Mrs. Throckhurst's interpretation had been valid," Miss Binns continued, "one might have expected your husband to check out books on coping with the problem of alcoholism in a dear one. He, of course, did not do so. The selection of books he did check out gave me a great deal of food for thought, as did his obvious elation when he returned the books two days later."

"I see," said Mom again.

"He had absent-mindedly left a slip of paper marking a certain page in one of the books, one of those dealing with snakes," added Miss Binns. "When I noticed that, I felt sure of the nature of his concern. I was quite certain your children had no pet snake that might be preparing to shed. And there were, after all, all those books about lizards and alligators and such to consider. Not to mention dinosaurs." Miss Binns again paused encouragingly, but when Mom said nothing she went on. "I know you to be a most sensible family. You would surely not be caring in secret for some normal exotic animal, an animal that would be better off in the wild or in a zoo. Still, I am aware that what I have come to believe would probably strike most people as fantastic."

"Oh," said Mom, so softly I could barely hear her. "Surely you couldn't think . . . . ."

"Well, you see," continued Miss Binns gently, "I had already guessed. I had not quite dared believe it at first, although I seldom doubt the evidence of my own eyes. I am an avid bird watcher, you know. My dear, your children have been wonderfully careful, but even so.... . Once or twice on Thursday afternoons, when I happened to be at my window with a pair of binoculars, they neglected to pull the shades.... Oh, my dear, don't look so alarmed. I'm quite sure no one else knows."

I remembered watching Drag glittering in that shaft of sunlight as she swooped for the beanbag. The shades—yes, we must have forgotten. Probably more than once or twice.

"I suppose," Miss Binns finished calmly, "that your dragon must be growing far too large to be comfortable in the house much longer. I am so glad you have that capable Mr. Martin to help you prepare more spacious quarters for her." She paused. "But I hope you will forgive me for asking about the one thing that puzzles me: why are he and your husband building that long counter against one wall?"

Chapter 9

"Jason," said Mom. "You might as well come into the living room."

"Oh!" said Miss Binns, as I entered. I hadn't expected her to look embarrassed. After all, I was the one who had been eavesdropping. But then she had thought I was in the garage—and probably she wasn't used to being wrong about anything. She quickly recovered herself and added, "Good morning, Jason."

"I think perhaps the others should come in too," said Mom. "But —"

I guessed right away why she might be hesitating. There needed to be some excuse to bring Dad and the other two in without Flash. "There's some lemonade in the refrigerator," I suggested. "I could take a glass out to Flash and tell the others they have to get their own if they want some. They'll be thirsty; they'll come."

"What an ingenious lad!" said Miss Binns. Mom,

who was still looking dazed, nodded. I figured the nod was about the lemonade, not about how smart I was, so I went out to the kitchen to get it.

As I had expected, everyone was thirsty. Once they were in the kitchen, I broke the news. "Miss Binns is in there. With Mom, in the living room. She knows." I figured Mom could tell them the other stuff, about her drinking problem and all.

Dad blinked.

"She knows about Drag?" said Rose.

"Miss BINNS knows?" said Philip. He looked hard at me, trying to figure out some way that it was my fault.

"No matter what," said Dad wearily, "the lemonade is a good idea." So we took the pitcher and a tray with glasses into the living room. Dad said a cautious hello to Miss Binns, and we all found places to sit while Mom poured lemonade for everybody. Rose carried the glasses around. Then everybody sat there sipping lemonade, waiting for someone to start.

Mom finally said simply, "Miss Binns is aware that we have a dragon, and she was wondering what the workbench is for."

So Dad said it was for making kites and told Miss Binns about our plan. I'm not used to hearing Dad sound nervous.

"I see," said Miss Binns when he had finished. "Most clever; a bold idea."

There was another awkward silence.

You could see Miss Binns wanted to say something else, but she hesitated. I never thought I'd see Miss Binns have trouble finding the words to say anything. Finally she turned pink and asked in a very soft voice, "Do you think I might be allowed to see her? I've only had glimpses."

"Rose," said Mom. "she's in your room. Could you bring her in?"

Drag didn't try flying down the hall; she was too big now. She came padding down it from the bedroom, just in front of Rose. As she came through the doorway, though, she spread both her wings wide and then to my astonishment glided straight to Miss Binns, landing just in front of her. She touched her chin to Miss Binns' knees, and the two of them looked into one another's eyes, neither one moving.

Miss Binns' cheeks were still pink, and when she spoke again it was still in that soft voice. "Thank you." She looked around at us. "Thank you for sharing her with me. I have read so many books, you know." She blinked her eyes quickly a few times, reached out one hand and gently stroked Drag's neck.

I didn't realize Mom had been holding her breath, but just then I heard her let it out—and she ran over to Miss Binns and gave her a sort of hug. It wasn't easy, of course, what with Miss Binns being in the chair and Drag right in front of her.

Miss Binns smiled faintly, gave a dainty sniff and managed to pat Drag's neck and Mom's hand at the same time. Then she felt in her purse for a handkerchief and dabbed her eyes. "Yes, dear, you really can trust me," she said, in a more normal voice. I couldn't be sure whether she was talking to Mom or Drag. "I may even be useful."

"What can you do?" asked Rose. That would have sounded rude if one of us had said it, but kids who are really little can get away with anything.

Miss Binns responded simply, "At the very least, I can be your sentry." She smiled faintly. "You already know that I am observant. I assure you I know how to listen as well. Almost everyone comes through the library. It might surprise you how often people do confide in me or let things drop without intending to. If anyone begins to suspect that something extraordinary is hidden in your home, I assure you I'm most likely to learn about it."

I remembered Dad's nickname for Miss Binns. Well, it might be safer to have Lady Long-ears on our side, at that. Also, I got the impression that Drag liked her. That gleaming green head was still resting on Miss Binns' knees—although it shifted a little each time someone new spoke, so the amber eyes could watch the speaker. The librarian turned to Mom. "I can also easily deal with that gossip," she said. "My suggestion is that I tell Mrs. Throckhurst that you mentioned to me how upset your children were by the decline and death of a pet goldfish."

Everyone else looked bewildered, but Mom said, "Ingenious."

"Furthermore," added Miss Binns, "although the plan you describe is an admirable one, I'm not sure you have actually thought through every last detail. Perhaps I can help with further refinements. How, for example, do you propose to transport Drag into the countryside for these flying sessions? She could not fit comfortably in the trunk of a car, even if that were a humane idea. If you attempt to hide her on the floor of the back seat— well, she will soon be far too big for that, too." Miss Binns shook her head briskly. "She'd show."

"I was thinking we could use a rental van," said Dad.

Miss Binns shook her head more gently, a smile on her lips. "Oh dear, no, that wouldn't do at all. People would first wonder whether you yourselves were moving, and when it turned out you weren't they'd become curious. You have no idea how people do notice things that are unusual."

Mom gave a peculiar laugh. "She's right, dear," she said to Dad. "Wait until I tell you about my drinking problem."

"Huh?" said Dad.

"I'll explain later," said Mom. "Do you have a solution to the problem of getting Drag out of town, Miss Binns?"

"Do call me Amelia," said Miss Binns. "I think that now that we are co-conspirators, so to speak, a certain amount of intimacy is appropriate. And may I call you Margaret and Andrew?"

Well, Mom and Dad are used to having their friends call them Peg and Andy, but I guess they decided Miss Binns had a thing against nicknames. They said in unison, "Of course."

Miss Binns looked pleased. "In public, of course, it would be wise to retain our usual formality. Well, returning to the question of transport, I myself can only see one solution—and I think it would be a generally helpful step. You must bring Mr. Martin into our—well, perhaps I shouldn't call it a conspiracy. You must bring Mr. Martin into our circle."

Tell Flash? I hadn't expected this. Dad had said we shouldn't even tell our best friends—and we had one extra person in on it already now. Miss Binns herself had just been talking about how to keep things secret. Still, it didn't sound like such an awful idea to me. In fact, as my surprise faded, it didn't sound like a bad idea at all. "Could we?" I said.

"I'd trust Flash," said Philip, the mature Voice of Authority.

"I LOVE Flash," said Rose. As though that were the point.

"I think we all trust Flash," said Dad. "But frankly, keeping a dragon a secret is surprisingly stressful. I'm not sure it's a good idea to inflict that stress on a friend unless it's really necessary."

"Maybe it is necessary," said Mom slowly. "He's going to help you make the kites, right?"

Dad nodded.

"Well, imagine how he'd feel if you go off and test them without him. That would be inflicting something on him, too."

Miss Binns beamed at Mom, like a teacher who is proud of a student for coming up with a right answer. "And it's not just a question of Mr. Martin's feelings, or the convenience his van offers. Remember, it will be known that both of you are involved in manufacturing these kites. It would be the natural thing to include Flash in their testing. I must continue to stress how important it is that everything appear as natural as possible."

"Amelia," said Dad, "I think you are going to be a very valuable member of our circle. All that makes perfect sense. Are we ready to decide it this fast? Does everyone think we should let Flash in?"

We all nodded.

"You know," admitted Dad, "it will actually be a relief. Keeping secrets from Flash is hard, and it never felt right anyway."

"Things are moving a little fast," said Mom, "but I guess we'll just have to ride with it. And it's funny—it would feel better to me, too, to let Flash in on things.

Let's see—Jason, go ask him if he'd like to come inside for a little more lemonade. But I think someone should take Drag back to one of the bedrooms until we've had a chance to explain. We'll want to break things gradually."

Flash was just finishing fitting the top for the work-bench when I got to the garage with my message. "Sure, more lemonade sounds good," he said, pulling off his bandanna to mop his face and then tying it on again. "I'm ready for a break, anyway."

"Miss Binns is inside, too." I figured this counted as part of breaking things gradually.

Flash pulled his T-shirt over his head. "I'm not sure I'm fit company for a lady right now," he said, looking down at the dark places where the shirt was still wet with sweat.

"It's okay," I said, "she knows you've been working. She's not really—you know, fussy." I knew that wasn't the word I wanted, and I wasn't sure why I was wanting to make sure he didn't think of Miss Binns as a prissy fussbudget. I hadn't ever thought much about Miss Binns as a person. I had only been worrying about keeping Drag a secret from her. I had certainly never wondered about whether I liked her. But something had clicked into place when I saw her looking into Drag's eyes. I understood why Mom had felt like hugging her.

Flash scowled at me and gave my shoulder a little shake as we walked together toward the house. "Miss

Binns," he said, "is NOT fussy. She likes to express herself precisely, and she has her standards." He finished up the shake by clasping his hand warmly to my shoulder. "People sometimes make fun of people who are different. Miss Binns is a real lady."

I had never thought before about whether Flash liked Miss Binns either, but it sounded as though he did.

Well, once we were inside it was Miss Binns who did most of the explaining, and she did it clearly. I realized that when you express yourself precisely, as Flash had put it, it doesn't take long to tell a lot of things.

"You don't even seem surprised!" said Dad to Flash once everything had been laid out for him.

"Oh, I'm surprised, all right," said Flash. "But I've seen a lot of surprising things in my time. And I've been getting a feeling there was something you weren't telling me. It feels good to be on the inside." He smiled suddenly, his eyes traveling quickly to each one of us. "Thanks for trusting me." He drew a deep breath. "And now—do I get to see this dragon?"

"May I bring her out?" asked Miss Binns.

"Of course," said Mom. "She's in the boys' room, on the left."

Miss Binns returned a moment later with Drag following just behind her. As they entered the living room, Flash rose to his feet. Miss Binns, her cheeks pink again, stepped to one side and stood there proudly, one hand on Drag's neck. Drag sat up on her hind legs and spread her wings to their full width. Framed against the doorway, she looked really huge.

I was starting to understand that being introduced to a dragon is a big deal for people. Flash stepped toward Drag and Miss Binns, dropped to one knee and swept off his bandanna again—flourishing it as though it were a hat with a plume. "I am here to serve you," he said. It sounds dumb telling about it, but trust me, it was an impressive gesture. Flash might look like a pirate, but he certainly knew how to act like a knight.

Not the kind of knight that kills dragons, of course.

Chapter 10

It's a good thing summer vacation started about then. I don't know how I could have made myself go to school during those next few months. Now there was more than a dragon at home. There were kites to be built, and Flash was around most of the time.

Dad and Flash argued happily as they bent over Dad's sketches. "Kites are like sails," insisted Flash. "Maybe I didn't spend my youth designing kites, but I learned a few things that year I spent skippering a boat down in the Virgin Islands. Listen to me, if you just allow for more movement here, you can decrease this area and make room for extra surface THERE where you want it. . . . "

It was fun to listen, but I liked actually working on the kites best. Dad needed the kite ribs perfectly smooth, and even Rose learned to help sand them. The three of us kept at it until the slender rods were satin to our fingers. Everyone helped with something. In the evening, Miss Binns would slip over quietly from next door. She and Mom would spread bright, thin fabrics over the dining room table and cut them. Then, with Mom's sewing machine on the table and Miss Binns' sewing machine on the desk, they both could work at once, stitching the skins that would be stretched on the kite-ribs.

Miss Binns was on a first-name basis with Flash now, the way she was with Mom and Dad. But she didn't call him "Flash"—she used his real name. When I heard that name the first time, I couldn't believe it. It certainly wasn't the kind of name I expected Flash to have.

"Percival?" I said as soon as I could get him aside. No way would I tease Flash in front of anyone. I may be hard on Rose sometimes, but she asks for it. "Your name is PERCIVAL?"

Flash shrugged. "My mom was a great reader." He glanced back at Miss Binns and then gave me his fiercest look. "SHE gets to call me that," he said. "No one else. To the rest of you, I'm Flash, got it?" I nodded.

Drag was growing faster and faster; we moved her out to the garage, where she'd have more room to move around. She had her third shedding the same week that we finished the first model kites. We celebrated her new set of scales and the kites that next Saturday: our first Flying Day. Dad had found a perfect place, an abandoned farm about thirty miles from town. There was a big field there, hidden from the main road by forest. The owner lived out of state, but Dad got a letter giving us permission to use it as our test ground. We decided that until we were sure that no one would come in while Drag was in the air, the grownups could take turns standing guard along the dirt road that led to the field.

I was worried that we wouldn't be able to make Philip get up when the alarm went off at five that Saturday, but he surprised me. He may not have been really awake, but at least he got out of bed and into his clothes. We bolted down some breakfast and were ready to go.

At exactly 5:30 Miss Binns tiptoed over from next door. Flash backed his van as close to the garage as he could and opened the back. Dad pressed the remote opener, and the garage door slid up. The rest of us were in the garage with Drag, ready to guide her into the van in case she was nervous about getting in. But Drag seemed to understand exactly what was needed—she hopped up and inside before we had a chance to do anything.

Dad rode in the van with Flash. We closed up the garage and the rest of us went to where Mom's car was waiting in front of the house. Miss Binns gave a swift glance up and down the block. "Good," she murmured, "Not a sign of life anywhere. They're all still asleep." She climbed in the front seat with Mom, and the rest of us piled in back.

Halfway down the dirt road that led into the farm we met Flash, waiting on foot. "I'm going to take the first shift standing guard," he said. "You shouldn't miss this."

"Percival," protested Miss Binns, "you should be there; you helped make those kites!"

"Everyone helped," said Flash. "And it's not the kites that are going to do the important flying. Go on—it's no use arguing. I'll have my turn."

The two kites we were testing that day were the Firebird, a real beauty, and the Spinning Lure—one of the designs that kept changing shapes and colors. Using pieces of meadow grass of different lengths, we drew to see who got to fly the kites first. Miss Binns and Rose were one starting pair, Mom and Dad the other.

Dad had opened the back of the van to give Drag more air. The three of us kids climbed inside to keep her company, while the grownups put the kites together. If Drag had really stretched out she would be longer than the back of the van, so she had to keep her tail curled a little. Still, there was really plenty of room inside. I sat on one side of her, Philip on the other. I always liked leaning against Drag, feeling the slight motion of her breath. Rose inched herself up Drag's tail, trying to get up on her back. "You think you're the lucky one again because you drew a long piece of grass," I told Rose. "You're going to be busy flying a kite. Philip and I get to watch Drag fly; that's the best." Rose stuck out her tongue at me.

"Rose gets a turn to watch too," reminded The Voice of Authority. "We're going to have all day. We'll all get turns at everything." Philip could have saved his breath. Rose wasn't bothered, just going through the motions. She knew I was going through the motions myself. The sun was up now and shining in the open door of the van, and a slight breeze carried in the smell of warm meadow grass. It was comfortable, leaning against Drag's side. Rose had managed to wriggle up to where Drag's wings started and was lying there face down. After a while she leaned over toward my side and whispered, "Philip's asleep."

Well, at least he had stayed awake long enough for us to get him out there.

"Okay," Dad called. "All set up!" Rose slid down Drag's other side, and I could hear her trying to get Philip awake again.

The one part of our plan that we couldn't control or predict was here. We knew by now Drag was super-smart, of course. We were pretty sure she understood why we were doing all this—that it was important to stay near us, important not fly out where anyone could see her. But we couldn't be certain. What if she got excited about flying and started heading off away from the kites?

But what could we do? Hope, and take the risk. No matter what, Drag had to have a chance to fly.

Rose finally had Philip awake again, so she hopped out and ran over to hold the Firebird. Miss Binns was going to run that kite up. Mom was holding the Spinning Lure. "Ready?" called Dad. "Go!" He and Miss Binns started off. Miss Binns could run faster than I expected, and she didn't need to run far. The kites were designed so that they almost wanted to fly. In seconds, both were high in the air. "Okay, boys," yelled Dad. "Drag's turn!"

We each gave Drag a pat, and Philip gestured with his head toward the sky outside. Drag needed no urging. She slipped from the van onto the ground, spread her wings, and pushed off.

Well, I had seen her fly indoors, but this was different. She hadn't been able to do anything you could call real flying since back when we had played keep-away with a beanbag. She was huge now compared to the size she was then. On this new scale, those acrobatics in the air made me catch my breath.

And her colors! Each new set of scales had been richer in color, more jewel-like, than the last—so those colors in the sun were even better than I had dreamed, from the beginning, that they would be.

At last here she was, above our heads, flashing in the sunlight. It was real. All the work, all the planning and secrecy and worry didn't matter. We had a real dragon in the sky above us—soaring, dancing, gliding. What I had told Rose was true: I really was lucky—it wasn't just that I was here to watch it happen, I knew I had helped make it happen. Finally, our dragon was flying free in the sky.

"I'm going to trade places with Flash," said Mom. She had come up behind me without my noticing it. "He should see this." She set off for the gate to the road.

It was hard to take my eyes from Drag, but after a while I began to notice the kites as well. They, too, were swooping and dancing. Drag was pretending to play with the Firebird now, flying circles around it, hovering beside it. The Firebird was made of silk that had a metallic look, and its tail had streamers of orange and scarlet and gold. In the sun it looked like a tail of flames. Curving close to Drag's glowing blue and green, the kite looked spectacular too.

And Drag did understand what she needed to do. She did. No matter how fast she flew, she always curved back in time, never went past the tall trees that hid this meadow from the highway. It works, I thought triumphantly. Our plan works.

At noon we pulled the kites in, called Drag down, and had lunch. No one had tried to come down the road all morning, and we decided we'd hear a vehicle coming in time to get Drag into the van—so we all just ate out on the meadow together. We agreed that we could probably forget about having anyone stand guard. We poured out Drag's food first. Mom had shifted her from canned food to dry, saying it was better for her teeth and gums. Drag must have been hungry after all that flying: she gobbled down a huge panful of the stuff before the rest of us were even half started eating, and then stretched out to rest. All three of us kids used her for a backrest—Rose beside her neck, Philip and me against her side. Mom eyed us as she finished her sandwich. "Andy, I think your next designs should be on a larger scale. Drag gets longer each time I look at her. If we want her to be taken for one of our kites, we have to make big ones."

"Well," said Dad, "We've got a new one almost ready to go that's bigger than these two."

"Thinking of the Dragonfly?" asked Flash.

"Right." Dad turned to the rest of us. "It's going to be of metallic cloth, too as close to Drag's colors as we can get. We've designed it so that it will be able to do a lot of stunts in the air."

"That would be a good name for a kite company," said Mom dreamily. "The Dragonfly Kite Company."

I blinked. And she didn't want Dad to take this idea too seriously? But watching those kites in the air had apparently made dreamers of everybody.

"If we could really start a company and sell our kites for a lot of money," said Philip, "we could buy an island somewhere, just for us. We could try out the kites there all the time, so people would get used to seeing them off in the distance. And Drag could fly any time she wanted to. People wouldn't be able to tell she wasn't just another kite."

"We could call it Dragonfly Island," said Rose, "because there would be a dragon flying there. Only nobody would know."

"How would we get to school?" I asked.

"Well, I'd be helping your dad," said Flash, "and I'd have a powerful motorboat to carry supplies back and forth. I could take you to the mainland each morning and pick you up each afternoon."

"Sometimes the weather might be too stormy to make the trip," said Miss Binns. "I think on such occasions it might be useful to have a governess." Even Miss Binns was sounding dreamy. "Occasionally I have wished that I could have been a governess instead of a librarian. There is a rich literary tradition of persons in such roles eventually having most interesting lives." She suddenly smiled. "Perhaps that could be my chance—as governess of Dragonfly Island?"

"Ah, Amelia, we'd happily engage you as such!" said Mom.

"Could Drag stay, then?" I asked. "If we had a place like that?"

There was silence. Miss Binns glanced toward Drag, as if expecting her to answer—but Drag didn't move, and her breathing was steady. She was probably asleep. "I wonder," Miss Binns said finally. "She does seem attached to us, and I'm not certain she feels a need to live with her own kind. It is not clear that dragons ever live in groups, actually. I don't remember a single tale that involves more than one dragon at a time."

"Well, mama dragons and daddy dragons would have to get together, or there wouldn't be any baby dragons," pointed out Rose. Rose understands the basics.

"But that doesn't mean they'd stay together as a family," said Mom. "For example, not all birds mate for life. Some do; swans, for instance. But not all. Just one encounter between a rooster and a hen is enough so that afterwards egg after egg will hatch into a chick. The rooster isn't really involved in the hen's life, except for that one moment."

"Turtles don't even hang around to watch their eggs hatch," contributed The Voice of Authority.

"There can't be many dragons left," mused Flash. "I wonder how they find one another, even for one meeting?"

"They find one another," said Miss Binns. "However unlikely it may seem, they do."

I felt Drag's solid back just behind me. Her egg, the one she hatched from, hadn't come from nowhere. Another dragon had laid it and left it on our doorstep, so to speak. Somewhere in the world there must be other dragons... .

"Is everyone going to sleep?" demanded Mom. "Come on, how about a little more flying?" A ripple of excitement ran through the scales against my back.

Maybe Drag hadn't really been asleep at all. I wondered if she, too, had been daydreaming about islands, about other dragons.

Chapter
11

That first Flying Day pretty much wore us out. From dawn until dark is a long time, especially out in the sun. We talked about it and decided that in the future it would be a good idea to bring books and cards and games. And everyone would spend part of the time in the shade resting.

But Drag never seemed to get tired, that day or any of the ones like it that followed. She just got hungry. Now that she was getting more exercise again, she was eating like a hog. No one was surprised when she shed for a fourth time not long afterward.

"These scales are made of LEAD," complained Dad as he folded the old skin and carted it off to the box in Rose's closet. "And I think this one fills up the second carton. Sure you want to keep saving these, kitten?"

"Pretty soon your whole closet is going to be full of old scales," I pointed out. "You won't have room for any clothes. You'll have to wear Drag-skins around."

"You said I could keep them," Rose reminded Dad. She was learning to ignore me—which kind of took the fun out of teasing.

It was right after the fifth shedding that we hit a major problem—one we should have seen coming.

We kids were all out in the garage watching Dad and Flash put the finishing touches on a new design. It was a hot day and almost time for dinner. None of us felt like doing much. I was up on Drag's back, sprawled out on my stomach; Philip was sitting with his back to her side, reading. Rose was snuggled in next to Drag's neck and had pulled the gleaming head around to her lap. Drag must have been tired or bored too. She was definitely asleep. You could tell. Now and then she would twitch, the way a dog does when it's dreaming.

Suddenly Rose gave a squeal. "Ow! Drag BURNED me!"

Flash and Dad stopped and turned. Dad looked puzzled. "BURNED you, bunny?" Dad is always calling Rose by animal names.

"All of a sudden her breath got all hot," whimpered Rose. "Well, maybe it didn't burn me, but it was HOT."

Drag was awake now, of course—Rose had jumped up as she squealed, letting Drag's head fall to the floor.

Philip scrambled to his feet and put his hand in front of Drag's nostrils. "Her breath is exactly the same as always," he said after a minute. Voice of Authority.

I slid down. "All the books talk about dragons breathing fire. I bet in her dream Drag was flying and shooting fire from her mouth. So that even her real-life breath started to get hot."

Dad and Flash stared at each other, and Dad ran over and lifted Rose up and hugged her to him. "Sure you're not really burned?" he asked anxiously. Rose nodded.

Flash walked slowly over and stood in front of Drag. Drag looked up at him. "Okay, babe," said Flash. "You were asleep. Not your fault. But we need to know. It's the way it is in the books? You can shoot fire from your mouth?"

I'd already pretty much guessed that Drag understood what we said—but what happened next proved it. Drag stepped backward, getting as far as she could from us. She opened her mouth—and very gently breathed out a flicker of flame. "Oh, brother," groaned Flash.

Dad was thinking fast. "She can control it," he said, "except when she's asleep and dreaming. But this garage is full of wood. Let's face it—she could burn the whole thing down in her sleep."

Flash was ready with a solution. "We could build a fireplace in the corner," he said. "with a big metal hood. Put a brick hearth in at floor-level. If she could sleep with her head more or less inside, her breath would go up the chimney."

"But you can't build that in a few hours," objected

Philip.

I was doing my best to think faster than anyone. "Remember there's that big fire-ring we made out at the field, so we could roast hotdogs? So far absolutely no one has ever come while we've been there." I was working out the rest while I was saying that much. The rest was the best part. "You could take me out there with our tent and leave plenty of food and water for me and Drag, and we could stay there while you guys are building the fireplace. I could stand guard in the day, and at night I could make sure she sleeps with her head in the fire-ring so her breath can't burn anything."

"That may be the best place for her to sleep until we can get some kind of fireplace in," said Dad, "but even working fast it would take us a couple of days to finish it. And you just aren't old enough to camp out there by yourself. Even Philip wouldn't be."

"Not even with a dragon?" said Philip hopefully.

"Not even with a dragon."

So we had another family conference. It was combined with dinner. Mom had made spaghetti, and you can always have extra people when you have something like that. Flash was already there, of course, and Mom called Miss Binns over the minute she saw her return from the library.

Dad explained the problem to her while Mom dished out the spaghetti. "Oh dear," said Miss Binns. "I'm embarrassed; I should have thought of that.

Virtually all the accounts do mention the fiery breath. But since it wasn't present earlier. . . .It just didn't occur to me it might develop as the dragon matured."

"I bet she's been able to do it for a while," I said. "She was probably trying not to, around us."

"Could be," said Dad. "The thing is, how do we keep her from burning things down until we can make a fire-proof corner for her? Jason suggested he could camp out with her at the flying field, so she could use the fire-ring there—but he couldn't be there by himself. All apart from his being a bit young to camp alone, there should be an adult around in case there are tres-passers."

"You and Flash need to build the fireplace," said Mom. "I could go with him. Then the other kids could come too."

Philip and Rose exchanged a triumphant look, and both turned smug faces to me.

"I should not advise that, Margaret," said Miss Binns. "Assembling provisions for such a large party would be difficult on the spur of the moment, and Rose might be likely to tire of the adventure rather quickly. Surely, moreover, you realize that for you to disappear precipitously, while Andrew remains here, would invite notice. And that is always what we must avoid." She smiled at me. "If you are willing to accept me as a camping companion," she said, "I should be happy to accompany you." She turned to Mom. "My library colleagues will not be surprised if I call in to take a few days' sick leave. Yesterday's story hour was badly attended, and we were all remarking that there is some kind of flu going around. The absence of my car will not be noticed, as I normally keep it in the garage."

Mom looked doubtful. "Amelia," she pointed out, "there's no . . . that is, there are no facilities out there. I'm not sure that you're used to roughing it."

"There is a stream in which to wash," said Miss Binns. "We can bring safe drinking water." She lifted her chin with determination. "There are ways of coping with other needs in the wild. I was an enthusiastic member of the Campfire Girls in my youth; I shall greatly enjoy the experience."

I don't think any of us had imagined Miss Binns as the roughing-it type, but she sounded pretty sure of herself. What could we say?

"It would be useful if Andrew and Percival could let us take the Dragonfly model with us, so that we can fly it during the day," added Miss Binns. "We should use this emergency excursion to offer Drag some further exercise. I have been concerned that our infrequent sessions are really not adequate for her needs."

Dad nodded, and to my amazement everything seemed to be settled. I tried not to look at Philip and Rose; it would be mean to gloat. Mom and Miss Binns rounded up enough food to keep us going for at least three days, and they put everything that might spoil in an ice chest. As soon as it was dark, we loaded that in Miss Binns' car along with food for Drag, the tent and sleeping bags, and all the other camping gear Mom could think of that we might need. Dad and Flash disassembled the Dragonfly and stowed that in the car too.

When Miss Binns emerged from her house, she had changed from her usual neat dress into blue slacks and a sweater. Her hair was in a long braid in back instead of a bun. "Ready, Jason?" She still sounded like the Miss Binns I knew, but if I put my eyes out of focus I could imagine what she might have looked like when she was a Campfire Girl. She still wasn't very tall, after all.

Together, we slipped out to where her loaded car was waiting. We waited to let Flash pull the van out of our own driveway and get a head start, then silently set off for the flying field.

"Sure you two will be okay?" Flash asked as he unloaded the food and camping gear. "Let me set up the tent for you, at least."

"You are most gallant," answered Miss Binns before I could say anything. "It would, however, be good experience for Jason and me to do it ourselves. I'm quite looking forward to this adventure. Don't fret, Percival. Things are indeed becoming more complicated, but this little camping trip is not itself a cause for concern."

Flash shook his head, ruffled my hair, and smiled. "You take good care of this lady," he said. A few minutes later the lights of his van disappeared into the woods.

Above us the stars were brighter than I had ever seen them, but down where we were it was suddenly awfully dark. "How will we see to put up the tent?" I asked.

"If the woods are thick enough to hide headlights," said Miss Binns, "They will certainly hide a fire. Drag, dear . . . ."

I could hear the two of them moving over toward the fire-ring. Suddenly their figures were illuminated by the warm glow of flames. Drag was resting her chin on the largest rock of the ring and gently breathing flames into the center. Darkness returned each time she had to breathe in, but those intervals were brief, not much more than the shadowing when an eye blinks. "In the morning we'll find some wood so we can keep a fire going steadily tomorrow night," said Miss Binns, "but this will do while we set up the tent."

"How did you get her to do that?" I asked.

"Oh, Drag and I understand each other," Miss Binns answered vaguely, busily clipping together the sections of tent pole. I pulled out the pads that would cushion our sleeping bags, opened the valves, and let them fill themselves with air. I still didn't see how Miss Binns had done it. She hadn't said anything to Drag. I would have heard if she had.

I wanted to stay up and try roasting some marshmallows on Drag's breath, but Miss Binns was firm. "That will work better when we have wood that can turn to coals," she said. "And it's later than you realize. Time to sleep."

In the middle of the night I woke up and peeked out the tent flap. The moon was up, and I could see things better now. Gradually, the silvery meadow came into focus. I looked over toward the fire-ring, to check on Drag. I squinted, looked harder. "Miss Binns!" I felt over toward where her shoulder should be. Good, there it was. "Miss Binns!"

"Yes, Jason?" One thing about Miss Binns, she was easier to wake than Philip.

"Drag's not there! She's gone!"

"She has simply left for a little midnight flying," said Miss Binns. "It's risky, of course, but the need to take risk is increasing rapidly. She'll return to the fire-ring. She understands fully about the need to prevent fire. She'll be there in the morning." Miss Binns reached out in the darkness of the tent, found my head, and gave it what I knew was meant to be a reassuring pat.

Miss Binns might be right—she usually was—but I was still uneasy. Even if Drag were back by morning, I was sure that this time she had gone beyond the flying field. People might see her. But I couldn't keep on bothering Miss Binns; I could tell by her breathing that she had gone back to sleep. It would have to wait until morning. Finally I managed to go back to sleep myself.

Chapter 12

Well, of course Miss Binns was right. When I woke up in the morning Drag was asleep with her chin resting on that big stone, breathing into the fire-ring the way she was supposed to. But when I tried to get her out of the way so that I could build a fire there, it was like trying to wake Philip. So she DID go a long way off, I told myself grimly. Probably flying most of the night.

After lighting the fire so we could heat water, Drag fell back asleep. I sipped my instant hot chocolate and ate a granola bar, watching her uneasily. Well, at least there aren't many planes at night, I tried to reassure myself. And up high, without sun shining on her, she'd be dark like a bat. People on the ground wouldn't notice. People don't notice bats.

But if she forgot and breathed flame . . . .

To my surprise, Miss Binns didn't say anything at all about Drag's night-time disappearance. For some reason it made me feel funny to bring it up if she didn't mention it. I couldn't see any way that talking about it was going to make me less worried, anyway.

After breakfast, we washed the dishes together in the stream and then went into the forest to collect wood for that night's fire. By the time we were back, Drag was finally really waking up, so we gave her a late breakfast. Then we set up the Dragonfly kite and spent the rest of the morning taking turns making it dance in the air with Drag.

The Dragonfly was definitely the best kite ever. It had a set of double wings made of iridescent plastic—transparent, but with colors skimming over the surface, the way they do on soap bubbles. Its silk body was as long as Drag's but slimmer, and the colors were nearly as beautiful as hers. You could make it do tricks by jerking the string different ways. Seeing it in the air with Drag was almost like watching Drag play with a younger dragon, one with a different shape, a different sort of wings. For a while, I forgot to worry.

After lunch Drag seemed sleepy again—and to my disgust Miss Binns said I should have a rest too.

"Even Rose doesn't take naps any more," I protested. "I don't need to rest."

"One doesn't always sleep soundly while camping, Jason," insisted Miss Binns. "I didn't say a nap, I merely said a rest. I'll rest as well." There didn't seem any polite way to refuse, so we pulled our sleeping bags over to the shade of a tree and lay on top of them silently. I didn't have my eyes closed, though—I was watching Drag through my lashes.

Miss Binns did have her eyes closed, but I could tell by her breathing that she wasn't asleep. I finally decided I needed to bring up some of the things that were on my mind. "How did Drag know you wanted some fire to see by? You didn't say anything to her. And how were you so sure about her coming back? She couldn't tell you what she was going to do."

Miss Binns didn't answer immediately. "It's difficult to explain," she said finally. "I told you we understand one another, and that is the best way I know of putting it. I could perhaps say that we can read one another's minds, but that is certainly not accurate. I have no idea of most of what may be in Drag's mind, although I am sure it would certainly be fascinating to explore a dragon's thought processes and memory. And I can't flatter myself that Drag would in general care to rummage about my mind, even if that were possible" Miss Binns paused once more. It seemed that even she was having trouble finding the words to describe this "understanding" precisely. "But from time to time she and I seem able to communicate, when one of us needs to tell the other something."

I knew Miss Binns wasn't the sort who makes things up, but I was having a hard time understanding how this communication worked. "You mean you hear her voice inside your head?"

"Oh no," said Miss Binns promptly. "Not a voice at all. It's somehow more direct than words would be. From time to time, I find that I simply know what she wants or feels, in a very vivid way. And it appears to work in the other direction equally well."

I closed my eyes and thought about that. I could remember a lot of times when Drag had seemed to understand what we said. But if Miss Binns were right, maybe she had understood the thought before we had even put it into words. That could make sense. "Okay, so she got the idea about staying close to the kites, and breathing fire, and lots of other stuff," I said. "But ...." I continued thinking, remembering, trying to find a time when maybe the communication ran the other way.

"But she's never let you into her mind?" said Miss Binns gently.

"Yeah," I said, trying to keep my voice from showing that it mattered. I knew I was being a bad sport, but it just didn't seem fair that Miss Binns was the only one Drag talked to. Or whatever I could call this talking-without-talking they seemed to be doing.

"I expect she will," said Miss Binns.

Oh sure, I thought. Sure. Pat me on the head.

The surge of anger that was washing over me didn't make sense. Miss Binns hadn't done anything mean. But I couldn't remember feeling that mad even at

Philip—and he always gets everything first.

We lay side by side a long time without talking. It finally seemed easier to go to sleep than try any longer to sort things out, so I did.

I must have dreamed, because just at the end of my dream, there was this kite that turned into a butterfly, and then the butterfly was trying to land on my face. When I opened my eyes, Drag was there touching my face with the tip of her green tongue. "Okay, okay!" I told her. "I'm awake." I looked around for Miss Binns. She had moved over to where she could lean against the tree and was reading. "Can you help me get the kite back up?" I asked. "I think Drag wants to play with it some more."

Even if Drag wasn't letting me into her mind, at least she did want me to do something with her.

Once I had the kite string pulling against my hand and was watching Drag circle the Dragonfly in the air, I felt more like myself again. Dad and Flash could take their time with that fireplace, as far as I was concerned. And if Drag wanted to communicate with Miss Binns, well, that was their business, after all. I was relieved I hadn't said anything more about that—glad that Miss Binns looked happy too, reading there under the tree.

Dinner that night was all things I really like. Drag lit the wood we had gathered, and once it had burned down to coals we barbecued some chicken from the ice chest. When it was ready, we ate it along with macaroni salad made with lots of pickle relish, and carrot sticks. For dessert, of course, toasted marshmallows. Later Drag led the way to the stream and breathed out just enough flame so that we could see to wash the dishes. I could tell she was being careful not to singe any of the nearby plants.

Every camp should have a dragon, I decided.

When we got back to the fire-ring, Miss Binns put the sleeping bags back into the tent. "I'm going to bed early," she announced quietly. "You and Drag will want to sit by the fire a little." As she disappeared into the tent, she said something that made no sense at all: "I'm not sure I fully approve, but it appears to be necessary."

I blinked, wondering if I had heard her correctly. But Miss Binns always pronounces her words distinctly; there was no mistake about what she had said. I shrugged. At least the first part made sense, so I went over to sit with my back against Drag's side and watch the glowing coals. If Miss Binns wanted me to stay up a while, I was happy to stay up.

And that was when it happened. If even Miss Binns couldn't find the words I probably shouldn't even try, but I will anyway. She was right: I didn't hear any voice or anything. Something more like a light, or maybe a sound my ears couldn't hear, and it went all through me—and I understood. Drag was going to fly again that night, and this time she wanted me to go with her. I didn't see any pictures, but it was almost as though for an instant I knew an image that was in Drag's mind, something she wanted to happen. I was on her back, and we were high in the air. I wasn't seeing that picture in my mind myself—but I understood that Drag might be. No words, no pictures: I just understood.

Even in my excitement, I remembered to get a pail of water from the stream to put out the coals in the fire-ring. Dad had taught us about taking care of fires. Before I poured it, I glanced back at the tent—just beyond our circle of light, barely visible. I was willing to bet Miss Binns wasn't really asleep. She had known what was going to happen. And she didn't fully approve. Yet she had deliberately left me alone with Drag. She didn't approve, but she was letting us do it. Pretty brave of her, actually.

If you are going to be a dragon's friend, you have to be brave, I reminded to myself. I poured the water on the last of the fire and climbed onto Drag's back.

Chapter
13

I was careful about getting settled up there. I've ridden horses, and I know about holding on with your legs, but horses don't fly. Experimenting, I discovered that if I lay close to Drag's back I could hook my hands over the start of her wings, right where they joined her body. There was a nice curved edge there that just fit my grip. Even if she swoops, I thought, I can hang on. I gave one more wriggle to make sure I was secure—and I was ready. I knew I didn't have to say so. I didn't even have to think so in words. I just let myself feel it in her direction, so to speak, and Drag understood. Her muscles tensed for takeoff, and I pulled in a deep breath.

The speed of what happened next took that breath away. I was glad I had a good grip. There certainly wasn't anything gradual about takeoff. Dragons aren't airplanes; there wasn't any taxiing down a runway. Drag pushed with her hind legs at the same time that her wings caught at the air—and we were flying.

By the time I had my breath back we were already getting high and starting to level off. If the stars had seemed bright before, now they were really blazing. Somehow they looked bigger as well as brighter. The moon was almost full, and I could see Drag's neck in its light. That worried me at first, until I remembered that from below there would just be her dark silhouette; she would merge with the night sky. And that was lucky, because she was heading out straight, not circling around. I had no idea where we were going, but I knew we had left the meadow behind us.

It's hard to tell about that ride in an organized way, because my mind was trying to do a lot of things at once. If I'm honest, I have to say part of the time I was just gloating over what I was doing. Riding a dragon. Me, Jason, riding a dragon. A real dragon. Part of the time I was trying to memorize everything, so I'd never forget. The way things looked: the sky, Drag, the lights of towns now far below us. The feel of the darkness rushing by me. The pulse of Drag's muscles as her great wings beat steadily on either side of me. Part of the time I was wondering about where Drag was taking me, trying to memorize the patterns of lights below me so I could maybe figure our route out later, when I had a map. Then I was back to thinking how for once Rose didn't have all the luck, and Philip didn't get to do everything first. I was riding a dragon.

It was a while before I got around to noticing that I was getting pretty cold. I had on my windbreaker, but with the night air hitting me so fast I was still cold. I pressed as close as I could to Drag's back; that helped. I tried to keep counting the clusters of lights we passed, so I'd know how many towns we had gone over.

When we finally flew over a huge area of lights, I started to guess where we might be. The town we lived in was not that far from the coast. We had visited the city there next to the sea, the city where they might move Dad. I remembered that farther out, there were islands. Some of them had whole towns on them, and ferries ran between those islands and the city. Some had just a few houses. Some of the islands were smaller or farther out still, and those didn't have any buildings on them at all.

We passed over what had to be the city, and it looked as though my guess about where we were might be right. I could see just a few spots of light ahead; those must be the houses on islands. I noticed Drag was starting to fly lower and lower still. I began to think I saw moonlight reflected on the sea, but my eyes were watering from the wind; I couldn't be sure. And then I was sure. No lights from towns or houses now; just the sparkles of moon reflected by the waves.

We were going slower now, still descending. I raised my head, peering into the darkness, trying to make out where we were and what we were doing. Drag was coming so close to the surface of the sea that I wondered whether she were planning to land there. Could a dragon float like a water bird? But we continued skimming along, now only yards above the moon-spangled water. Looking ahead, I suddenly saw something massive that was blocking my view of the stars. We must be coming to one of the islands.

Drag kept going straight until there were almost no stars at all ahead. We were angling up a little now, but it looked as though if we didn't crash into a cliff we'd be landing on some kind of steep slope. Well, if I could get through that takeoff I could manage anything. My handholds wouldn't be much help in a sudden stop, though; I clung as hard as I could to Drag's sides with my legs.

But landing was different; it was as gentle as dandelion fluff drifting to rest. Drag's wings swiveled and changed beats, to brake us. I barely felt her feet touch down. She took a few steps forward and then lowered her body to the ground, inviting me to get off.

I carefully slid down her side to what felt like hard rock. It was totally dark. I kept my hand on Drag's side, not sure I could find her again if I stepped away. I couldn't see a thing—no stars, no light from the moon. Nothing. Nothing but blackness. Where on earth were we?

Dragons aren't human—but maybe they enjoy surprising people, the way we do. I can't think of any other reason Drag let me stay in that darkness for a minute before breathing a long plume of flame into the air before us. It illuminated the largest cave I had ever seen—a cave like a palace. The walls and ceilings sparkled with crystals, except where enormous pale curtains of stone, formed over ages, divided the space near the walls into smaller chambers.

I turned to see how we had come in. Behind us was the narrow entrance to the cave, and a shallow ledge on which we must have landed. Drag let the flames die, and now I saw stars framed in the tall, pointed arch of the opening. I could see the moonlit waters, too—but they looked hundreds of feet down. The cave must open into a steep cliff of some sort; there would be no way to get up to it from a boat.

Drag's breath illuminated the cave once more, but I was suddenly flooded with her impatience; she had other things she wanted to show me. I mounted again, and in the darkness she turned and slipped out the narrow opening.

I knew what a dragon take-off felt like now, so this time I wasn't caught by surprise. As soon as we were in the air we banked and turned, heading back for the island. But we didn't land there again. Drag just flew back and forth, keeping so close to the contours of the land that it was almost like riding a roller-coaster, only not so jerky. I wasn't scared exactly, but I certainly held on tight. I felt her wanting me to look at the island—

but it was hard to see much, even with the moon. I did figure out that the island was long rather than round. I could tell there were a lot of trees down there and with all that up and down there certainly were hills. One was almost big enough to call a mountain, and it broke abruptly into steep cliffs on the long side of the island where the cave had been. That part I could see pretty well. There was one place further inland where we just glided smoothly for a minute. I was pretty sure I heard the sound of a waterfall there, so I knew there had to be a stream somewhere down below.

I understood that Drag wanted me to memorize everything about the island. I wasn't sure, though, that I could keep everything sorted out and hang on at the same time. After all, I had been storing a lot of things in my mind during the ride out here. But I tried my best.

Finally Drag must have been satisfied, for her wings began to beat more strongly, and I could feel us rising toward the stars. Soon the island and the sea were below and behind us, and we were passing over the city lights again. I pressed myself as close to Drag's back as I could, my nose against her smooth scales. I was too cold to fall asleep, which was lucky, but I was tired. There so close to Drag, I hardly felt anything unusual was happening when she opened her mind wider to me. This time, though, what she was sharing didn't seem so clear. Maybe she was trying to let me know things that were hard for anyone but a dragon to understand. I only really understand one part clearly: that I must remember everything about this night, but for now I should save what I remembered as a secret. A time to tell about it would come, but for now I should keep the memory inside me. I was too tired to wonder why, but I did understand that much.

And of course Drag understood I'd do it.

Our landing back at the meadow was another gentle one. Drag continued on foot to where the fire-ring was, lowered her body again and breathed me some light so that I could see to get down. My legs—especially my knees—were stiff and chilly, and my hands felt almost frozen. I knelt beside her neck. Now that I had some practice, I could almost feel my mind opening to hers, letting her know what I needed. Immediately she breathed out just enough flame to let me warm my hands. Once they were warm I put my arms around Drag's neck for a minute, quietly, before I went off to my tent. I tried to open my mind as wide as I could to hers. I wanted her to know what it had been like for me, that ride, and I was certainly too tired to find a way to put it in words. It was good to know I didn't have to.

Miss Binns stirred in her sleeping bag as I slipped into mine. I was afraid she would try to ask me about where I had been—but she just went back to sleep. I had no idea what time it was, but I knew it had to be really late. Probably more like early in the morning. Tired as I was, though, I don't think I went to sleep right away. Memories of flying with Drag shaded so easily into dreams of flying with Drag that it was hard to be sure when I crossed the border.

Chapter

14

The funny thing was that Miss Binns never asked me anything. I was sure she'd cross-examine me at breakfast, but not a word. She just let Drag and me sleep late, and once we were awake she started frying eggs and pouring out dog kibble. Not one question.

At least it made it easy to do what Drag wanted about not telling.

That afternoon, while Drag danced in the air with her Dragonfly friend, I reminded Miss Binns, "You said something the night before last about Drag needing to get more chances to fly than we're giving her."

Miss Binns had her eye on the kite. She gave the string a little jerk, and the Dragonfly looped the loop. Drag followed close behind the kite, tracing larger circles. "Well, don't you think so? It can't be natural for a dragon to be as confined as she has been lately."

"Well," I said, "we can't fly kites every day. People

would figure out we're not just testing new models. Anyway, Dad has to go to work during the week."

"I believe," said Miss Binns, "that we are going to have to accept some new risks. But we should, of course, discuss this with the others." Before I could ask what she meant, she changed the subject. "Speaking of the others, I wonder if they can indeed complete the fireplace by the end of the day? I was considering taking the tent down, but it might be best to delay that until we are sure that construction has proceeded on schedule."

The fireplace project, it turned out, had gone so well that Flash came out to join us before it was even dark. He helped us pack, and stow the camping gear, and volunteered to be in charge of dinner. Dinner was scheduled to be hamburgers with all the trimmings. "Hey, there must be three pounds of meat here," said Flash, looking into the ice chest.

"Mom wasn't sure how long we'd be out here," I explained. "She wanted to make sure we had enough food, in case the fireplace took an extra day."

"Well, let's grill some for Drag," proposed Flash. "I know she likes that dry food okay—but we can give her a little people-food for a change. As chief fire-maker, she deserves a share." It sounded good to me. I got ready to put mustard and relish and everything on the buns for Drag's hamburgers, but immediately got the message that dragons don't go for that stuff. Miss Binns must have felt Drag's reaction too. She gave me a funny quick smile, the kind of smile that would have gone along with a wink if it had been anyone else. Drag ate six hamburgers—with buns, but of course no trimmings—and all her regular food as well.

After dinner we roasted the rest of the marshmallows, one by one. No one was terribly hungry any more, but we were in no hurry to get going. Drag lay quietly, breathing a little flame on the coals from time to time to keep them hot. Between marshmallows I watched the fire's reflection in her amber eyes. If you could really go all the way inside a dragon's mind, I thought, it might be like that cave. Big and mysterious and full of places to explore.

Flash and Miss Binns, seated together on the other side of the fire-ring, were pretty quiet, too.

Finally Miss Binns made a little shrug, stood up, and said, "Well, time to pack up the last things. It's quite dark now, and we can drive back." So we did.

Miss Binns closed the car in her garage without unpacking it. "We can unload things later," she said. "I dare say your father and Flash are eager to show off their handiwork."

Everyone was there inside the garage. "Ta-DAH!" sang out Dad as we entered. Drag lay stretched diagonally across the garage, her head on the new brick hearth, her nose pointing straight in—as if to show everyone what the new fireplace was for. Tiring of that pose, she lifted her head and curved it back so she could flick her tongue across Rose's hair. Rose was gleefully scrambling all over Drag, and no one seemed to be noticing that it was already past her bedtime.

"I helped make it," said Philip, gesturing toward the fireplace. "Especially the brick part. Flash showed me how. I mixed all the mortar myself. And set a lot of the bricks."

I started to say "Big deal!" automatically, but stopped. Okay, he got to do that stuff—but I had been on Drag's back up there among the stars. I knew how I'd feel if Philip had got to ride her and I hadn't. So I quickly changed what I was going to say into, "It's great."

"This garage is starting to turn into a family room," said Mom. "We're spending more and more time out here, and now it has a fireplace. Do you think there might be room for an old sofa over at that end?"

The Voice of Authority chimed in immediately. "There isn't much room for Drag to move around as it is," Philip objected. Actually, he was right.

"That brings up something I'd like to discuss before we break up tonight," said Miss Binn in her clear voice. Everyone's head turned. There was something about her tone that told Rose it was time to stop horsing around; she slid off and sat on the floor next to Drag. "During these last two days, watching the eagerness with which Drag has taken to the air has convinced me that we can no longer pretend to ourselves that our weekend expeditions to the country are enough," said Miss Binns. "She needs to fly—really fly—on a daily basis."

Mom and Dad both started to say something, but Miss Binns raised her hand. "I know the practical constraints. There is no way our kite-testing cover can be used that frequently. But as Philip just pointed out, Drag can no longer move within the garage in such a way as to afford significant exercise. I believe we must make it possible for her to fly from the garage at night and simply accept the risk that involves." Miss Binns hesitated, glancing at me. "Drag herself has made the decision to take greater risks; she did so two nights ago."

Everyone looked startled. I was surprised for my own reason: Miss Binns hadn't mentioned that Drag had taken me along the second night. "She left the regular flying area?" asked Mom.

Miss Binns nodded. "I cannot, of course, say for certain where or how far she went, but I am quite sure she flew a considerable distance. A growing dragon needs such extended flights; we must face that realistically. We'll of course want to continue to offer her such protection as we can—but not at the cost of her freedom and health."

"People will see her!" protested Rose.

"Perhaps not," said Miss Binns. "As long as she

remembers not to breathe fire, once she is in the air she should be nearly invisible in the night sky. I expect she knows how to avoid altitudes where she would encounter airplanes. The driveway from which she will be taking off is well-shielded by your house and my own, and this is a quiet street. I believe that once it is dark, she can come and go without major risk of being seen."

Mom frowned. "She probably does need to be free to fly," she said, "but I still don't see how we can work it. We could let her out once it's dark—that part's easy. But we'd have no way of knowing when she returns. It would be in the middle of the night, and we'd all be asleep! How would she get back in?"

Dad sighed, his face sober. "We always knew we couldn't keep her forever. Maybe it's getting to be time for her to be on her own. She's pretty big, after all. We should probably be trying to help her find someplace where there aren't any people—someplace in the wilderness, where she might not be discovered."

"We can't just dump her somewhere," objected Philip. "She's never had a chance to learn to hunt for her own food. She'd starve."

"I don't think we need think in those terms at this point," said Miss Binns, "nor have I any reason to believe Drag wishes to leave us. We simply have to be willing to live with more risk. As you say, Margaret, she can easily leave the safety of the garage as soon as it is dark. If you will lend me a remote opener for your garage door, I will be responsible for letting her back in and closing the door once she is inside. It will be no trouble. My house is sufficiently close to your garage so that I can do so from my bedroom window."

"But you'll be asleep!" protested Philip. "How will you know she's there wanting to get in?"

"I shall know," said Miss Binns firmly.

"She'll know," I said.

Dad started to say something, then stopped. He and Mom looked at each other, then at Miss Binns, then at me. Philip and Rose just looked at me. Flash was behind me, so I don't know where he was looking. But he was the first one to speak. "I have a strong hunch these two know what they are talking about," he said. "I guess we just start living dangerously. And I guess we might as well start now. Where do you keep your spare opener, Andy?"

Chapter 15

After that, Drag went out every night, and as far as I could tell she stayed out for hours every time. I usually woke up when she came back—I guess I could feel her needing to get in, the way Miss Binns could. Always, a minute after I woke up I would hear the faint sound of the garage door opening and closing, and then usually I'd go back to sleep. But one time she stayed out so long I never fell asleep once she was back. After I heard the door close I lay awake, thinking. Wondering where Drag went when she flew—whether she went back to that island, or just flew around for exercise, or whether maybe she was looking for something. Wondering whether Someone would see Drag, and what we'd do if

Someone found out she was here. Wondering whether Drag would leave before that happened. And whether she'd ever come back, if she did.

Once you start worrying about one kind of thing it's hard to keep the other things that are bothering you from popping up too. So I found myself starting to wonder, too, about whether Dad's company was still talking about transferring him, even if he hadn't mentioned it for ages. And before I could stop myself from worrying about all this stuff I noticed it was starting to get light—so I just let myself go on worrying until it was time for breakfast.

I don't suppose Drag was out quite that long very often, though.

Philip of course never woke up the way I did, but he still figured out that Drag's flights weren't short ones. "Drag is sleeping half the day now," he pointed out to me. "She must be staying out for hours to be that tired." We all could tell from what was happening with her appetite that she was finally getting enough exercise. I don't think any other animal grows as fast as a dragon. In August, she shed twice. There was no more room in Rose's closet for the skins, and anyway these bigger ones were too heavy to move far. Flash and Dad just shoved them to a corner of the garage.

I don't know whether it was because Drag was asleep so much, or because she was getting to be so big—but I was starting to be less certain about how

Drag was connected to us. It's hard to explain what I mean. I do know it had stopped feeling like having a pet. She was ours—but she wasn't ours. She was a dragon.

When I could see and touch her I felt safer. I don't think I was the only one. Philip usually spent his afternoons, now, reading with his back against Drag's side. Rose brought a lot of her toys out to the garage and staked out a territory in the curve of Drag's tail as her place to play. Since Drag was getting so much exercise outside, Mom had gone ahead and put a couch in the garage. In the early evening Mom and Miss Binns sewed or read or talked together, while Flash and Dad worked on new designs at the workbench. Drag would be awake by then, but she'd just lie there quietly, the gaze of her amber eyes going from one of us to another.

Of course we all kept worrying that someone would see her. The library got newspapers from all over the state, and Miss Binns was checking them carefully for any sign that Drag had been sighted. As August neared its end, there had been only one item to concern us, and it had been earlier in the summer. There had been reports of a UFO over the city—and the date of the sighting was that first night of our camping trip, the first time Drag flew away from the field. Different people had reported different things, but they all mentioned irregular flares of light in the sky. "I should imagine that dragons can get excited too," admitted Miss Binns. "Drag may have forgotten her normal

111

caution, and let herself breathe flame." It could have been coincidence, of course, and nothing to do with Drag. And at least no one could connect that UFO with our town, with us.

I had this feeling, though, that something was going to happen. But nothing did—until the end of August.

The first warning came in a call from Miss Binns. The phone rang after breakfast, about the time the library opens. I was the only one in the house just then, so I answered it. "Jason," Miss Binns said quickly and softly. "There's an item on the second page of The Herald your family must read. I believe you subscribe to that paper? I must return to the front desk. Goodbye, dear." And she hung up.

I found the newspaper, opened it to the second page and saw right away what she was talking about. I have to admit I never read much of the paper except the comics, but I don't know how Mom and Dad missed it.

I raced to the garage with the paper folded open to the second page. Good, Flash was there, too. "Look," I said, thrusting the paper into Mom's hands. I guess my voice showed how upset I was because Flash and Philip both stopped what they were doing to read over Mom's shoulder, and Rose put her doll on the floor and watched us with wide eyes. Mom read the article aloud, so Rose would know what was going on.

The Beat of Pterosaur Wings– Or Just a Flap?

An amateur astronomer with interests in paleontology has reported sighting what he believes to be a pterosaur, flying in the night skies above our town. Carl Williams, of 71 Owens Lane, estimates that the creature has a wingspan of at least 20 feet.

"I hesitated at first to report what I saw," confessed Mr. Williams, "knowing that no one would take me seriously. I am, however, quite certain of my observations. There are no known night-flying birds or mammals with such a wingspan. Moreover, I am sure that the creature I saw had well-developed hind legs. It could not possibly have been an owl or a bat."

Howard Cowgill, leading paleontologist at the state university, was more cautious. When contacted by *The Herald* he was quick to assure us that the report by Mr. Williams had not been treated lightly when presented to his department.

"We have the greatest respect and regard for observations by dedicated amateurs," Dr. Cowgill told our reporter. "Nevertheless, we do feel that the most likely interpretation of the sighting by Mr. Williams would be a bat flying somewhat closer to his lens than he realized. His impression that the creature had large hind legs, even if correct, would not actually support his interpretation. Recent theory in our field, based on the remains of a *Sordes pilosus* now in possession of scientists in England, makes it doubly doubtful that pterosaurs would have had legs of the relative size and development reported. The absolute size of such creatures was actually relatively modest, in any case -- not on the scale that Mr. Williams' remarks would seem to imply."

"Uh oh," said Philip.

"Someone saw her?" asked Rose.

"It looks that way," said Mom. "But at least it doesn't seem that either this fellow at the university or the reporter at the paper took it seriously."

Flash grinned. "Poor Mr. Williams," he said. "From now on, he's branded as a nut. But he saw what he saw, and he got it almost right."

"And he did see her." I shook my head. "You can bet he'll be trying to do it again. Probably there are plenty of other people around with telescopes who will halfway believe him. They're all going to start looking."

"When Dad gets back we can talk about whether Drag should lay low for a while," said Mom. "Flash, can you stay for supper? I'll call Amelia and invite her."

"You should start charging me board," said Flash. "I've been eating with you folks almost every other night. Can we at least do it as a barbecue, with the steaks on me?"

"We could have a night picnic," suggested Philip, "out at the flying field. That way Drag could be there too, and we'd have room. It's fun to barbecue after dark, anyway."

"You kids wouldn't really want to wait until dark to start eating," said Mom. "But we could compromise. Nibbles and salad here around six, to keep us from starvation. Then when it gets dark we can go out into the country for steaks and roasted marshmallows." She breathed a deep breath in, and then blew it out with a windy sigh. "I'll phone Dad so he'll know what's going on, and call to make sure Amelia is free."

It wasn't until she left to phone that I noticed that although Drag hadn't moved during all this, she hadn't been asleep. Her eyes were open.

I moved over next to her, sat down, and shut my own eyes for a minute, trying to figure out what was going to happen now, what we could do. I finally gave up; I didn't know. Then I tried hard to feel for what Drag was feeling or thinking—but whatever that door was that sometimes opened between us, it was almost closed. I got a faint sense that she wanted to comfort me, but it felt mostly as though she were busy with her own thoughts, dragon-thoughts.

Chapter 16

It was a strange day, that one. The weeks before had already felt like a kind of waiting—and of course, now we were still waiting, but it was different. Now it felt as if something was starting, but it wasn't clear what. I wanted to know. Even if it was bad, I wanted to know. I knew there was no way to make time stop, just stop, stay where it was, so that Drag's solid side would keep on being there right behind me, my back keep on rocking a little with the in-and-out of her breath.

I guess everyone was feeling the same way. It was a sunny day outside, but we mostly stayed in the garage. Philip and I pretended to read, one on each side of Drag. Rose climbed onto Drag's back, carrying one of her dolls. Sometimes she played with it in the flat space between the wings, but a lot of the time she just lay there, holding the doll. I noticed at one point that she was sucking her thumb. She hadn't done that for more than a year.

Mom had brought some of the ledgers out to the garage, but it didn't look to me as though she was getting much work done on them. She left to make sandwiches for lunch and carried them back to the garage so we could eat there. Flash left for a while too, going out to buy the steaks. Most of the time he was there leaning on the workbench, his boots wrapped around the rungs of his stool, the designs for a new kite in front of him. From time to time he'd draw or erase a line.

No one said much.

Miss Binns got there before Dad did. By the time he came, Mom had already brought celery sticks and pieces of cheese out to the garage for everyone to munch. "Sorry," said Dad, "I couldn't get away. There was a long meeting at work." He gave Mom a kiss and stroked Drag's neck. I searched his face hopefully. But if Dad had come up with some great new plan for handling this next stage, it certainly didn't show. He looked really tired.

I saw Mom look at him too and then away. "You must be hungry," she said. "I'll get the potato salad." She went out to the kitchen.

I'm not sure how hungry any of us felt, but everybody ate the potato salad. As long as we were eating, we could put off talking about things. Finally Miss Binns put her fork down firmly and cleared her throat. "It is, after all, merely one local sighting," she said, "and it is unlikely in itself to be taken seriously by anyone. But it does remind us that any dragon living in a town is most unlikely to remain a secret forever. We must think realistically about the future."

"Do you think Drag is ready to be on her own?" asked Philip.

"It could be she has learned to hunt her own food during these nights out," suggested Flash. "We don't know."

"I doubt it," said Mom dryly. "Not given the amount of food she's eating here."

"I don't see how we could teach her how to hunt, anyway," said Philip. "We don't know anything about hunting ourselves."

"Drag wouldn't like to hunt and kill things," said Rose. "I think she likes what we feed her better."

It was a perfect opening, but I didn't make a crack about how Drag would actually love to eat a tender maiden like you-know-who. I just sat there.

Dad hadn't said anything at all since he started on his potato salad. Now he lifted his head and looked around the circle. "I'm afraid that Mr. Williams and the others with telescopes are not actually our most urgent worry," he said. "Sorry I have to break this right now, but putting it off won't help. There's something else that's going to make it hard to keep Drag much longer. That meeting today at work was about the future plans of the company." I saw Mom's eyes close for a couple of seconds at this, but no look of surprise on her face. "They have definitely decided they do want to make me an administrator," Dad continued. "The transfer is on." He paused and lowered his eyes to the floor. "They understand we'd need time to sell our house and find a new place to live in the city, so my new duties don't need to start right away. They suggested something like six months—longer, if we have trouble selling the house."

Mom didn't say anything; she just reached for his hand and held it.

The first one to find words was Miss Binns. "I know this new position is not the heart's desire," she said gently. "Is there any possibility that our fiction of starting a kite business could become a reality? I have some savings I could invest in it, if that would help."

"Me too," said Flash instantly. "And if we started the business somewhere out in the country, that could buy more time for Drag too."

Dad lifted his head and looked at each of them in turn. "I'll never forget that you offered," he said, "but I can't even think about accepting. It's a risky venture at best, and not the sort of thing to let friends sink their life savings into. Anyway, I doubt that even between all of us we'd have enough cash." He smiled faintly. "I admit, I've been getting serious about the idea." He lifted Mom's hand in his, looked at it a minute, and sort of fiddled with her fingers as he continued. "Peg was willing to take the plunge if we could scrape together what we'd need. She knows I've been trying to feel out possible backers lately." He sighed. "But the ones that have real money aren't interested, and the ones that are interested don't have real money." With one last pat, he put Mom's hand down. His voice became very quiet. "I have to face facts. At least for now, the thing is a pipe dream. And I don't foresee any miracles during the next few months."

Rose was trying hard to follow all this. "We're going to have to move?" she said. "And we can't take Drag, or Miss Binns, or Flash?"

"It looks that way," said Mom.

"What happens to Drag when we move?" persisted Rose.

Even the Voice of Authority didn't have an answer. "We haven't figured that out yet," Philip finally told her.

I wasn't surprised to see Rose's thumb go back into her mouth.

Chapter 17

If you think about it, Philip was being optimistic. What he said to Rose implied that we were going to be able to figure something out once we worked at it.

Once it was dark, we did go out to the flying field the way we had planned—but it was the gloomiest barbecue in history. Even the fact that Flash had brought along chocolate and graham crackers, so that we could turn our roasted marshmallows into s'mores, didn't help.

Before we started there, we had agreed that our job now was to think of ways to help Drag learn to get along alone and of some place safe we could take her to live before we had to move. So, as we ate, we tried. We managed to come up with a few ideas about places, and that was all. But each idea, once we talked about it, turned out to be not so good.

I thought about that island, of course, but I didn't

mention it. First because I wasn't sure the island was really one where no one lived, second because I understood I wasn't supposed to tell about it right now, and third because Drag already knew about it anyway. Before long we ran out of ideas about places, and no one ever had any ideas about helping Drag learn to hunt. Things wound down, and we just sat there, looking at the fire.

Finally Mom spoke. "I guess maybe it's not up to us. Maybe we've been all the help we know how to be. Maybe now it's up to Drag. After all, the fact that she exists shows that dragons have learned to survive—that they do survive, even in this modern world. Surely she's nearly full-grown now. I guess we just have to hope she will know how to fend for herself when that becomes necessary." Her voice started to sound funny and tight. "Because there should always be dragons." I crossed my fingers, hoping she wasn't going to cry. I had only seen Mom cry once, and I had hated it. But she drew a deep breath and went on in a more normal voice, "Remember, she's been doing a lot of flying. Maybe she's already found her own place to live, when she's ready to go. Or when she has to go."

I thought about the island again. Maybe that was what it was for. We all turned to look at Drag. She was quietly breathing flame onto the coals of our bonfire to keep them going. Her amber eyes reflected the glow. I remembered watching them that night after she took me up on her back, and again I wondered what a dragon's mind would be like inside.

"Margaret is right," said Miss Binns. "At this point, we should try to accept the idea that Drag is wise enough to make her own choices and needs to be free to do so."

"Even about whether to go on flying right now, when people are probably looking for her?" asked Philip.

No one said anything for a second, and then Mom and Dad spoke at the same time. "Yes," they said together.

So that was that.

After a few minutes of silence, we started to pack up the food and stuff. Dad went to get some water to put out the coals. As he was coming back, Drag quietly rose to her feet. She unfolded her wings, stretched them for a minute, and then folded them once more to her sides. Quickly, she curved her neck to touch each of our faces with her tongue, then stepped back, spread her wings once more, and took off. "Well, it looks as though she's not giving up on flying," said Flash. "Safer from here than from the driveway, anyway."

Nobody else said anything. Nobody said what I was afraid one of us might say, or asked what I didn't want anyone to ask. We tried to follow Drag with our eyes, but soon there were just the stars. Finally Dad poured the water onto the coals. The steam going up, pale in the moonlight, hid the stars.

Flash and Miss Binns rode back in the van, we in our car. On the way back, Mom tried to be comforting. "We knew she couldn't live in our garage forever," she pointed out. "And we have kept her safe so far. We still have six months before we have to move. She's a strong dragon now, ready to find her own life. Even after we move to the city, maybe we'll see her again. It's not impossible. We all know by now that she understands what is on our minds, and some of us can understand part of what is on hers." I blinked at this. Did Mom know how to do it too, or had she just figured out about Miss Binns and me? But Mom went on. "Who knows—if we take vacations out in the wilderness, Drag might somehow know and come to meet us there."

"It's not just Drag," said Philip. "Miss Binns and Flash are like family now. If we move, I'll miss them."

"We'll all miss them," agreed Dad. "But we'll stay in touch. We'll see them again. That's a sure thing."

"It won't be the same as having them around all the time," said Rose.

"No, it won't," said Mom. "But they will always be our friends. Well, more than that. Philip said it right. They will always be family. Together, we seven have been a dragon's family. That is something, remember. Not many people get to be that."

"And we did keep her safe," Dad reminded us again. "Remember the Someones we thought might take her away? Well, they didn't. And I don't think they're going to. I don't think they can, now. Whatever else happens from here on out, I don't think that will happen."

But none of this seemed to help much the next morning, when Miss Binns phoned at breakfast to let us know that Drag hadn't come back during the night.

I had tried hard not to think about whether Drag was saying goodbye, there by the campfire. I guess we were all hoping we'd have a little more time together—even if the time was starting to feel like a long ending, more sad than happy. Whatever, now we knew. It had been goodbye, back there.

Rose got out of her chair and crawled up on Mom's lap. Mom held her close and stroked her hair. Philip and I tried to keep on eating. At least we didn't cry. For once, not even Rose was crying.

Dad finally said he could take a sick day and we could all go out and do something special together, but Mom said no, life was going to go on. "We are a lucky family," she said firmly, "and this is not the end of the world. Everyone understood Drag would need to go sooner or later. We'll get through this." She gave Rose's back a little rub and studied Dad's face. "Moving to the city won't be the end of the world either," she added. "We'll be doing it together."

I remembered what I had said to myself that night I flew. "Dragons' friends have to be brave," I told Dad, "and that's what we are. So don't worry about us."

Even Rose sniffed hard and tried to pretend she wasn't finally starting to get teary.

"What a bunch!" said Dad, shaking his head. His tone was half-joking, but I think he was really proud of us. And he did finally leave for work.

Mom read stories aloud to us for a long time, all of us snuggled together on the living-room couch. Afterwards, she spread out her work on the dining-room table so that Philip and I could play a game on the computer in the den. The game felt boring, though, and after a while we quit. Philip went off to his bunk to read.

I wandered out to the garage, without being sure why. Drag wasn't there any more. Even Flash wouldn't be there today. He had mentioned last night he'd be doing a job for another neighbor. But even if it was empty, the garage seemed a comforting place to be.

It turned out that the garage wasn't quite empty. Rose hadn't turned on the lights when she went in, but enough light was coming in through the little window over the workbench so that I saw her there. She was over in the corner where Drag's old skins were, sitting on the floor, sucking her thumb again. She had pulled one of the skins over so it was next to her cheek, just the way she used to pull up that ragged blanket of hers, and she was stroking it as she sucked. It was pretty pathetic seeing her turn back into a baby, but I didn't tell her that. I didn't know what I could say, exactly, but I went over and sat down next to her. She let me be there and even moved closer to me after a while.

The thumb-sucking got on my nerves, though. Finally I reached over and pulled her hand away, trying to do it gently. "Hey, let me touch that skin too," I said. "Don't hog it all for yourself." She sniffed and handed the part of the skin she had been stroking over my way. "A front foot, huh?" I said. "Look, at least we have that to remember her by. Good idea of yours, to save the skins." Well, it was a hard time. I can be nice to Rose in an emergency.

Then I looked more closely at what was in my hand.

"HEY!" I said. "Go turn on the light, would you, Rose?" She sniffed again, but without protest got up and went over to the switch. The big fluorescent bulbs above the workbench flickered and caught, and light flooded the garage. It glittered on the scales Rose had been rubbing. They weren't dull and yellowish. They were gleaming. They were gold.

Chapter 18

The first thing we did of course, was to try rubbing more of the scales—first with our fingers, then with one of Dad's shop rags. The dull, cloudy coating took some work to remove, but it did come off. Underneath, all the scales were gold. I kept rubbing while Rose ran in to get Mom and Philip. By the time they got there, some of the scales had come loose from the dry skin and fallen to the floor. Philip picked one up and bit it. "Don't eat it!" cried Rose in alarm.

"I'm not," said Philip calmly. "That's what they do in books to see if something is really gold."

"Does gold have a taste?" asked Rose.

"Pure gold is supposed to be soft enough so that if you bite hard, it leaves a print," explained the Voice of Authority. We looked at the scale in his hand. There was a little dent in the golden disk.

"I wonder if it could be?" breathed Mom.

"I think we should call Dad," I said. "I think we should call Miss Binns and Flash, too. I know they're all working, but they can think of some excuse to leave."

Well, I don't know what excuses they used—but they all got there pretty fast. We were polishing hard while we waited for them and pulling the scales away from the papery skin. By the time they came we had a whole gleaming pile of scales on the floor. They were round, like coins. Everyone peered at them, felt their weight, tried biting them. "Sure seems possible to me," said Flash. "I know someone who can tell. Want me to take one to him? It would only take about half an hour."

"Sure," said Dad. "As long as it can be done without explaining anything."

"This guy won't ask any questions," Flash assured us.

As the sound of his Harley-Davidson faded into the distance, Miss Binns raised her eyebrows. "I fear some of Percival's early acquaintances are not quite respectable people," she remarked. "But I must confess I myself have no contacts that would allow us the confirmation we need without problems. Perhaps dubious acquaintances can, on occasion, be a blessing."

While we waited for Flash to come back, all of us kept on polishing. The stack grew higher. Mom suddenly giggled and sang:

When a dragon's scales get old
Each one starts to turn to gold!

"Now, let's not all get too excited," cautioned Dad. "We don't know whether they're really gold or not."

Miss Binns had been unusually quiet as we worked, but now she stopped polishing and spoke. "I think it is highly likely they are indeed gold," she said. "It would explain a great deal."

"What do you mean?" asked Dad.

"It might explain, for example, why dragons became virtually extinct," said Miss Binns. "If at one time people learned that their discarded scales were gold, they might have assumed that the scales of living dragons were gold as well. We of course saw the change happening, although we did not recognize it for what it was. Those less intimately acquainted with dragons might assume their scales were gold underneath all the time, and the greedy ones would begin to hunt them down in hopes of becoming rich."

Philip interrupted, "And then dragons would have to hide in caves and start acting fierce."

Miss Binns nodded. "We know from personal experience that our own dragon has a nature that is curious, sociable, and at times even playful. I suspect that without persecution, most dragons would have been equally friendly." She nodded at the growing stack of gold disks. "There is another thing this phenomenon might explain. Has it occurred to anyone else?"

To my surprise, Rose was the one to answer. "The stories about treasures," she said. "A whole lot of fairy tales have gold treasures in them. There aren't any treasures like that any more."

Miss Binns beamed. "Precisely what I was thinking! All the treasures mentioned in folktales, all those pots of gold reportedly found at the ends of rainbows, all those caches of gold said to be under the guardianship of leprechauns—all such stories might be based on the discovery of cast-off dragon skins. Exposed to the elements, the skin membrane would decay and wash away in the rain, leaving the scales there as a heap of gold coins."

Mom nodded slowly. "I suppose those few discoveries made in modern times," she said, "could have generated the occasional reports of pirate treasure found in caves. Dragons and pirates are both associated with caves, after all."

That started me thinking about something, but before I could work it out, we heard Flash's motorcycle pull up and stop outside. He came bounding in the door, a big grin on his face. "It's the real stuff," he announced simply.

Mom closed her eyes a moment and shook her head. "Whoosh!" she said. "Now what?"

"We have a huge pile of real gold?" cried Philip.

"Plus," I reminded him, "two more cartons of the stuff in Rose's closet."

"So now what?" said Dad, grinning at Mom.

Mom grinned back. "Well, for one thing, I guess we

don't have to move to the city," said Mom. "And I guess we can stop looking for backers. Even part of this would be enough to set up the Dragonfly Kite Company."

"But how can we convert this to cash without explaining how we got it?" said Dad. "I don't think it's legal to own this much gold."

I stood up and spread my hands high to make sure I had everyone's attention. "I know!" I announced, once they were all looking at me. By now, I had had time to think things through. And I knew I didn't have to keep anything secret any more. This was the time. "We are going to have to move, though."

"I don't want to move!" interrupted Rose.

"Oh, I don't mean move to the city," I said. "Dad doesn't have to take that job." It was taking a lot of effort to keep on explaining everything calmly. I felt like yelling and dancing around. "Drag had it all figured out. You remember a long time ago when we were talking about having a Dragonfly Island? Well, Drag went and found one. It's perfect. She showed it to me. And it has a cave on it—so we can pretend we found the gold there. Everyone will think it was left by pirates."

Then I had to tell about everything, of course. I thought Philip was going to kill me when I got to the part about getting to ride on Drag's back. "Well," I pointed out, "I had to stay awake nearly all night to do it. Everyone knows you couldn't do that. And Rose was too little; she would have been scared."

"No I wouldn't!" Rose protested, but without much conviction.

"And the grownups would have been too heavy, even Miss Binns," I continued. "Drag wasn't anywhere near full-grown, back then." Well, there wasn't much Philip could say; I was right on every count.

"Are you sure you could find that island again?" asked Dad doubtfully.

"I know more or less where it has to be," I said. "And I know the shape it is, and about what size it is, and how one long side is the highest. I might be able to find it just by looking at a good map. But if I could see it from the air, flying low, then I'd be really sure. Because then I could find the cave. The opening is narrow, but I'd recognize it."

Mom pursed her mouth and shook her head. "That's going to be hard to arrange," she said. "You don't have Drag to fly on now, I'm afraid."

Flash threw out his arms and said, "HEY!" We all looked at him. "I'm no dragon, but I'll do! Didn't I ever mention I have a pilot's license? I spent two years flying a helicopter, and a helicopter is just what you need. We can get one. You can rent anything if you have enough money. And don't worry, I've kept my license current. Let me front the rental money. No, Andy, you keep quiet—we're not going to worry about anybody's life savings right now. Not with that stack of gold sitting in the corner."

Flash never says he can do something unless he can. The helicopter we rented had room for just four people. Everyone agreed that Philip and Rose should get the extra seats, because they had missed out on the ride with Drag. It was lucky we could go looking in person, because it turned out that on the map there were four different little islands that could have been it. The third island we checked out was the one. I could tell the minute I saw the slope of the big hill, and of course when we flew around to the side that faced away from the mainland, I could point out the opening to the cave.

There it was. Dragonfly Island.

Chapter 19

We had another family conference about how to plan the rest of it. Dad was reluctant at first to let Flash and Miss Binns add their savings to ours to get things started, but they argued him down. "We need to own that cave before we find the treasure in it," pointed out Flash.

"You cannot pretend there is any significant financial risk," added Miss Binns. "It would be a loan fully justified by the collateral sitting in the corner of this garage. I myself would suggest that you regard our contributions as investments in a joint venture rather than as a loan, but you may choose whatever arrangement makes you comfortable." So Dad gave in.

Miss Binns did the research to find who the island belonged to. Librarians know how to find out anything. It turned out the current owners had inherited the property, had never visited it, and had given up on trying to find a buyer for it. It was too small for a resort community and too far from the city for most people. They were delighted to get it off their hands. So that part was all right.

By pooling everyone's money, there was enough for the down payment on the island, the down payment on a big motorboat, and something left over to live on for a while. We all decided that since Flash was going to be the boat's captain, he should be the one to name it— and he christened it the *Lady Amelia*.

Well, I have to admit that I was secretly hoping that once we got to the island Drag would be in that cave, waiting for us. That would have made everything perfect. We couldn't look inside the cave, of course —it was too high above the water to get there from the boat, and there was no path down from the top. But as soon as we landed, I knew she wasn't there. I was calling and calling with my mind, and there wasn't any answer.

Even if things couldn't be perfect, they were pretty good. It turned out that there was an old building already on the island, a kind of hunting lodge left over from the last time someone had tried to stay there, years back. It wasn't much, just a couple of big rooms—but the roof had held up, so it was still solid. We didn't have enough money to build a real house right then, not until we "found" the gold, so we decided to fix up the lodge and start off by all living there together.

Dad resigned his job, telling everyone he was finally going to start the kite business they had been hearing about. Nobody asked questions. "They have more than enough people who want to take that city job," he told us. He grinned. "They all think I'm crazy."

"Are you sure you want to do this, Amelia?" Mom asked Miss Binns at one point. "There is only a privy, and we'll have to heat water to bathe."

Miss Binns smiled. "All my life," she said, "I have read books about those who were fortunate enough to lead adventuresome lives. At last I have a chance to be one of them. You forget, Margaret, I am a trained camper. There is, as you say, a privy; that is a significant amenity."

Before the weather started to turn bad in October Dad and Flash had managed to add two extra rooms to the lodge and a stone fireplace to the larger of the original rooms. The new rooms started out as bedrooms for Flash and Miss Binns. In the end, though, Rose got one of them for hers—because Flash and Miss Binns decided to get married.

Back when I first knew them, I would have said that was a crazy idea. Now that I knew them better, of course, I saw they weren't so different in the ways that count. The only problem I could see was what we kids were supposed to call Miss Binns after they got married. It would have seemed funny to call her "Mrs. Martin" when we just call Flash "Flash." But she must have seen the problem too. Just before the wedding, she gathered the three of us together. "You know," she told us, "sometimes Percival calls me 'Lady A.' as an affectionate nickname. I have never had a nickname before and find that I rather enjoy being so addressed. Would you children like to call me that, too?" So that was solved.

We let them move out to the island first, for their honeymoon, and the rest of us joined them at the beginning of November. We had been taking the gold out to the island little by little, a few bags each time the boat went out. It was too heavy to carry all at once. We had polished all the scales into coins except those of the first skin. We weren't going to sell that one; Rose wanted to keep it. For the winter, we decided, the gold could be stored in the lodge. We'd need better weather to get it into the cave.

That first winter was an adventure—no really bad parts, though, although our money ran out before it was over. Flash had to sell some of the pieces of gold to that man he knew, to get us through. Once spring came, we lugged the rest of the gold up to the edge of the cliff just above the cave. Dad helped hold a rope firm while Flash slid slowly down the surface of the cliff, bracing his feet against the rock, until he had reached the ledge at the cave entrance. He had a big electric lantern fastened to his head, so he could see inside the cave. Once Flash was down, we took turns lowering sacks of gold down to him, to stash away there. I let Rose help me when I was doing it. I didn't let her know it would have been easier to do it without her.

When the gold was all in place, we "discovered" it—and no one questioned our story. The government officials who came out could see that the cave was almost impossible to get to, and I guess they figured that was why pirates would have chosen it as a hiding-place, and also why no one had discovered the treasure earlier. They bought all the gold at its full value and even urged us to keep the whole story of our "pirate treasure" quiet, so it wouldn't get in the papers. "They don't want people to start tearing into caves all up and down the coast," explained Dad. "Most caves are at sea level, and a lot of them have sea lions living in them."

Flash and Lady A. just laughed when Dad tried to pay them back the money they had chipped in at first. "Sure, Andy," said Flash. "We'll take it if you want—but then you have to stop trying to make us take equal shares of what that gold brought in." Dad let it go—we were a family now, and it didn't matter any more whose money was whose. Anyone's share of that gold would have been more than enough to build everything we needed. So we started building.

By then we had discovered that we all liked the idea of living in one house. We built the new one with more rooms than the lodge, but after we moved in we usually spent our time in the biggest one, a gigantic room with a huge fireplace. The important thing, of course, was that now we had three bathrooms—all with tubs and showers both—and plenty of hot water.

Flash loved zooming around in his motorboat, but he told us firmly that people living on an island needed to know how to sail. "Until you know the feel of a sail or a rudder," he said, "you're wasting the sea." So we bought a sailboat too, a sloop. Dad got to name that one, and he called it Peg o' My Heart. Corny, of course, but Mom loved it. We went sailing almost every day. Flash was right about sailing.

Out in back, our new workshop was as big as a barn. We could store enough materials and tools so that even when the weather kept us cut off from the mainland, kite production could go on without a hitch. With all that building and sailing going on, we still got kites into production that summer and fall—enough to start us in business. Just as Dad had hoped, people went wild about them. We sold every kite we could make, and were already getting orders for the next Christmas season.

So it might sound as though this is the end of the story. It isn't.

I'm going to tell about just two more things, though.

The first one happened that Christmas. We didn't have much snow that winter, but it was cold. Usually I wake up first on Christmas morning, but this year everyone in the house woke up at once. I mean that literally. As I woke, I heard the bunk above me creak, and Philip say "HUH?" And I could hear Rose shrieking with excitement: "MAMA! DADDY!" I jumped out of bed and threw on my robe, and so did Philip. Flash and Lady A. were coming out of their wing, tying on their own robes, as the two of us reached the main room. Mom, with Rose in her arms, was already at the door with Dad. They were in flannel nightshirts; they hadn't even stopped for robes.

Of course Lady A. and I knew what had called us awake. I bet the others did too, even though it was their first time.

Drag was truly full-grown now, even bigger than when she had flown off from the campfire. But our main entrance had a tall pair of double doors, and when we opened them both she could squeeze in. Once she was inside there was no problem. That main room had a lot more space than our old garage did—enough so that Drag could move around just fine, once we shifted the furniture a little.

As soon as we could get calmed down, Drag let us all know what she wanted next. One by one, we bundled up against the cold, so Drag could carry each of us in turn to see the inside of her cave. Even Rose got to do it. I had seen the cave before, of course, but this time it felt different. Now it was Drag's, and she was back to stay. I had always known it would be the perfect place for a dragon to live: safe and secret and beautiful.

So from then on Dragonfly Island was exactly the way we had dreamed it.

There's still one more thing to tell, though, remember?

And that's the answer to the one part I didn't have figured out: why Drag had stayed away so long. That continued to bother me, even after she came back. I like to understand things. After all, she could have flown straight to the cave to wait for us. She knew that as soon as we found out about the gold I'd realize that it was meant to get us to Dragonfly Island. Right? So why didn't she just go there and wait?

That spring brought the answer. Early one morning Drag called us kids to come with her, and she took us straight to her cave. By that time Mom and Dad had decided it was okay for all three of us to ride her at once, as long as Rose was in the middle. Philip could reach around her to hang onto me, and his arms kept her safe.

As we slid off her back in the dim light from the entrance, Drag suddenly breathed into the air a plume of flame so enormous that it lit up the whole cave at once, making every crystal sparkle. What she was showing off, there on the cave floor, was a pale oval—luminous in that fiery light.

"Oh," was all Philip said. For once, he didn't try to tell us what we were seeing.

"Another one!" said Rose, running to claim it as hers.

Well, let her. I finally had everything figured out. Okay, so that was why! Drag had to go find a mate, first.

Because there should always be dragons.

About the Author

Alice
McLerran

An "Army brat" who spent her childhood and most of her adult life moving from one place to another, Alice McLerran may at last be ready to put down some roots. She has long wanted to live near the mountains or the sea. Now she has succeeded in doing both, by stretching her life between the two coasts of the U.S. She and her physicist husband now spend most of the year in a New York village near the Atlantic; their second home is in the mountains of Oregon.

Readers wanting to know more about the author and her books are invited to visit her website at: www.AliceMcLerran.com.